MASHER

Stormy Souls MC Book 5

BY

Payton Hunter

This is a work of fiction. Names, characters, places, and incidents either are the product of the author's imagination or are used fictitiously. Any resemblance to actual persons, living or dead, events, or locales is coincidental.

For more information, address:
paytonhunter.author@gmail.com.

First e-book edition December 2024
Book cover design by: Joetherasakdhi
Editor: Nicola Thorpe
ISBN print: 978-1-7385414-9-2
ISBN e-book: 978-1-7385414-8-5
www.paytonhunterauthor.com

ABOUT THE BOOK

Christmas is my favorite time of the year, and who am I to believe that the Stormy Souls MC isn't a family like any other, who celebrates Christmas as much as we all do. Maybe slightly different. I hope you'll enjoy reading this novella as much as I enjoyed writing it.

TRIGGER WARNING

This book includes scenes detailing explicit sexual acts, Christmas, and strong explicit language. It is not suitable for people under the age of 18 or people with triggers relating to any of the above.

ACKNOWLEDGEMENTS

Thank you to my editor, Nicola Thorpe. I would not have been able to do this without you.

Thank you to my family and friends for continuously supporting me. Thank you to my friend Tammy Carney, for your encouragement and unwavering support.

A special thank you goes to my Beta and ARC teams. You are the best!

DEDICATION

To my readers,

Have a very Merry Christmas and the best New Year.

STORMY SOULS MC CHARACTER LIST

Road Name	**Rank**
Raven	President
Vegas	Vice President
Slender	Sergeant at Arms
Pennywise	Enforcer
Dawg	Secretary
Clusseaud	Road Captain
Ferret	IT Guy
Moggy	Member
Sparks	Member
Ratchet	Member
Zippy	Member
Dougal	Member
Halfpint	Member
Striker	Member
Spen	Nomad
Greg	Prospect
Caleb	Prospect
Mom	Club mother, mother to Pennywise

Others

Neil	Bar Manager
Chris	Bar man, Security staff
Darcie	Therapist
Jade	Foster child of Dougal and Sarah
Amy Owens	Resident of Debs' Haven
Mel	Resident of Debs' Haven
Eve	Tattoo apprentice

Old Ladies

Chloe

Ashley

Ellie

Caroline

Terrie

Sarah

Ally

Raven

Vegas

Slender

Dawg

Clusseaud

Dougal

Sparks

Club Girls

Tequila

Ebony

Clarity

Restless Slayers MC

Fury	President
Ghoul	Vice President
Masher	Sergeant at Arms
Ghost	IT

Wild Pixies MC

Rainbow/Ally	President
Abby	Vice President
Jules	Sergeant At Arms
Tanya	Enforcer

TABLE OF CONTENTS

1 — MASHER

Stomping the snow off my boots outside my cabin, I hurry to get the key into the lock and into the warmth. Duluth is as cold as a polar bear's ass this year, but then it is December.

I still struggle to feel at home here some days, but I am grateful to have patched over, despite the guilt nagging at me once in a while, that I have dragged tensions with me.

When I made my decision, I knew Fury, my old Prez, wouldn't be happy, but hell, there's no way I want to be part of the direction the Restless Slayers are taking. Their shit weighed heavily on me, and I don't fancy ending up dead or in the pen. My daughter needs me too much right now, and to be honest, I need her too. She's the only blood family I have left. Although if I have my way, this will change, and pronto.

The last three months I've spent mostly supporting Tanya, and Pennywise, too. Now that I can do no more and must leave them to their own healing process as much as possible, I intend to make sure that the other reason for my patching over knows exactly that she's mine, and mine for good. I'm not taking no for an answer.

I never thought I'd fall in love again. Not after my Old Lady died soon after Tanya's birth.

I loved Tanya's mother, hard.

Rebecca was my everything. My sun and my stars. My universe rotated around her. After losing her, I fell into a deep hole, and only Tanya kept me from joining Satan of my own accord. For years, she haunted my every dream, every free moment of my thoughts. She'd have hated what I turned into. A jaded, hard man, only softened by the grace of his daughter.

My life revolved around the Restless Slayers MC, and being the best SAA they'd ever seen. To say I got my hands dirty puts it mildly. Some days it felt like they were dripping blood, even though I scrubbed them clean. I don't miss that bit, and to be honest, I'm happy to be just a patched member of the Stormy Souls.

Raven, Vegas, Slender, and Pennywise are doing a sterling job as officers, and I'm not getting any younger. At the ripe old age of fifty-five, I want to put my life right and put the woman I've fallen hard for in the place she belongs. By my side.

I walk into my room, toe off my boots, fold my cut and carefully place it over the back of my armchair. Grabbing my cell out of the inside pocket, I sit back into my "grandpa chair" as the boys call it, and shove my feet on the low table, staring at the pale flesh of my big toe poking through a hole in my sock.

Me: Hey, gorgeous, can I take you on a date tonight? It's been too long.
Hells Bells: Have you hit your head on the doorframe? A date? Tonight? It's freezing out! I ain't getting on a bike for love nor money!

I chuckle to myself as I read and reply.

Me: I'll pick you up at seven. In the club SUV.
Movie and dinner, what do you say?
Hells Bells: Okay. Don't bother picking me up, though, I'll meet you outside the movies. Seven sharp. I've got band practice until a quarter to seven anyway, so I'm in town.
Me: Okay, gorgeous, see you at seven.

Smacking my forehead, I berate myself for having forgotten she plays in a band. Not a good start, old boy, not a good start. Better pay attention from now on.

Damn it, I forgot to ask if the SUV is free! I really don't want to freeze my nuts off on the bike.

I dial. "Hey, Raven, is the SUV free tonight?"

"Let me have a look. Yes, one of them is. The other is in the workshop. Why are you asking?"

"Well, I want to take my future Old Lady out, if you must know. The problem is she doesn't know she's destined to be my Old Lady yet. I'd like to make that clear to her tonight."

Raven's booming laugh nearly deafens me.

"Masher, you dark horse, I didn't think you had it in you. Anyone we know?"

"None of your damn business," I grumble at him.

"While I've got you on the line, Masher, I'd like to ask a favor."

"Go on, Raven, shoot, whatever I can do to help."

"I'm so glad to hear you say that, though I'm sure you'll regret your willingness in a minute. Chloe and Caroline have been chewing my ear off. They want a proper Christmas party this year. With a tree, presents, decorations, the whole shebang. Thanks for taking charge of that. I appreciate it."

As I choke and cough, Raven howls like a hyena, throwing in the odd cackle.

"Keys for the SUV are in the garage," he says and hangs up on me.

For fuck's sake, a Christmas Party?

I look towards the heavens.

Why me? Tell me, why me? Who does he think I am, fucking Santa?

Huffing like a pubescent teen, I storm into the bathroom, slam the door, and take my time in the hot shower, slowly defrosting my ass.

And just like a pubescent teen, my dick stands to attention as I visualize my girl's long tousled hair and ample tits after I fucked her silly last time.

If you think you're getting my hand, you are sadly mistaken. The only way you get to feel it is me slapping you down. So down, boy!

Is he listening to me? Hell no. He's got a head of his own, that one. *See what I did there?*

I turn the shower to cold, which provides some relief.

Dressing in my best black jeans, button down, and boots, I chuck on my cut, and meander down to the clubhouse into the bar. Caleb is on shift and hands me a beer as I nod at him. He's an ace guy, and due to be patched in soon. Chris, our other prospect, is on door duty at Leather and Lace. Looks like we'll have to find some fresh blood soon.

To my surprise, Ferret is at the bar, stare fixed into his glass of amber nectar.

"What's up, man?"

"Huh?" He looks dazed as he lifts his eyes from his drink. "Nothing, just thinking."

He looks me up and down.

"Shouldn't I be asking you what's up? You look mighty smart for a rough old guy." He grins at me.

I slap him round the back of the head. "Oi, less of the old. You're only five years younger than me. I take offence, I have you know." I smirk at him.

"Don't remind me. I'm hitting the big five-o this month," he groans, rubbing his head.

Yup, been there, done that.

Turning around, I dig out my phone and check the time.

Holy shit, it's six forty-five! I'm gonna be late, and she'll have my balls, just not in the way I like it!

"Here, hold my beer." All the worst situations started with that sentence.

I trip over a chair, nearly face-planting into a table. Raucous laughter echoes behind me, at my expense, as I run out of the bar, down the path, into the garage. Ripping the keys from the board, I race back up to the SUV, only to find I picked up the wrong key. Crap! All the way back, running as though Satan's after me, I grab the right key this time, get in the SUV, start it, and haul ass out of the gate.

Tuning the radio, I discover that every, and I mean every radio station is playing damn Christmas songs. I'm not a bah humbug, but tonight could turn me into one.

I drive as though I stole it, literally, all the way into town, abandoning the SUV in the parking lot and racing to the cinema across the road, where my dark-haired beautiful woman nearly takes my breath away. Despite her planting her hand on her cocked hip, pointedly looking at her watch.

Before she can chew me out, I grab her and plant a hard kiss on her lips. She tastes like cherries and heaven.

"Sorry I'm late, honey. Forgive me?"

"After that kiss, how could I not? You might have to carry me in. My knees have gone weak." She flashes me a coy smile.

"I've missed you," I whisper in her ear, holding her tight.

"Missed you too, big man, so much." Her reply hits me right in the feels.

Reaching up, I undo her tight ponytail and run my fingers through her luscious, raven locks. I love it when she wears her hair down. She's very sure of herself and doesn't mind the few gray streaks peppering it. I adore the way she takes no shit, is fiercely protective, confident, and all woman. She's tall, almost my height, and I'm six foot two.

We've been seeing each other for a while now, on and off. Not for any other reason, as we both live busy lives. First, the distance was an issue, then Tanya and Pennywise got into trouble and we agreed concentrating on family was our first priority.

But now, the stolen weekends in seedy motels aren't enough. I want her, and I want it all.

She leans into me, molding her body to mine, pressing her hips against me, rubbing against my rock-hard length.

"Shall we skip the movie? I'm famished."

For a second there, I thought it was Christmas already.

“Sure baby, anything you want.” I smirk at her, and she swats my arm.

“Put that dirty mind of yours on hold. This lady here needs feeding first.” She winks at me.

Okay then, food it is.

2 — HELEN

The last three months have been hell on earth.

Most of the time I had no idea whether I was coming or going, and I frequently wanted the world to stop and let me get off, at least for a short while, to catch my breath.

I've seen more shit than I can handle, and the only way I've been able to cope is by throwing myself into my job and my music. The drums saved my life when all I wanted was to beat the shit out of something, but my true love is my saxophone. Belting out tunes, using all of my breath control, keeps me grounded, and knowing that at the end of a session I'll be exhausted enough to fall into bed and sleep. Sleep has not come easily, not for what seems like an eternity.

Masher's message this afternoon took me by surprise. Our meetings and contact had more or less stopped, but I understood. Tanya had to come first. I'm still not sure she's dealing with everything, but she's surrounded by love and empathy, which has to count for something, surely? Pennywise has been there for her, every step of the way. He loves her so much, and it's killing him to watch her upset without being able to do anything about it. He only started back at work four weeks ago. He says work gives him a break.

I must admit, I was a little pissed that Masher was late. But, man, that kiss? It swept me off my feet and sent my body haywire with emotion.

How can that man make me feel so pretty, wanted, needed and cherished, all in one kiss?

After Bear, I didn't think I'd ever feel anything for any man again, especially a biker. But fate had other ideas. Don't get me wrong, I loved Bear to distraction; he was it for me. So, when he died, I didn't believe it was possible to feel that deeply for another man. I'd given up on men and love. Convinced I'd never desire another man, the force of my passion for Masher took me by surprise.

Especially the physical aspect. I've been menopausal for a while, and as I understood it, moodiness and dryness are just two of the issues women my age go through. Imagine my amazement when I discovered the latter problem doesn't apply to me. Masher makes me so hot, my blood reaches fever pitch.

With too much time to think during those sleepless nights, I've wondered where we are heading, if anywhere at all. My decision came instinctively.

Tonight is D-day; I intend to let him know, in no uncertain terms, that I'm not his bedwarmer, or just a stopgap. I'm serious about him, love every aspect of him, but if he's not serious about us, we need to part ways now. Before this thing between us drags us along, chews us up, and spits us out the other end.

He grabs my hand and leads me to the SUV. I can't stop the laughter bubbling up when I spot he's parked across not one or two, but three spaces.

"Woman, no teasing; I was in a hurry," he grumbles with a smile.

"Did I say anything?" I cough to hide my giggles.

"Didn't need to, your smirk said it all." He snickers at me.

"Oh, you know me so well, caveman." I cackle as he helps me up onto the seat, leans over, and buckles me in.

"Where to?" he asks.

"Do you know the steakhouse just outside of town?"

"Sure, baby, it's on the right-hand side just after the town limits, isn't it?

"Yes, that's the one," I confirm.

"Let's go feed you then." He smiles, puts the SUV in drive, and gets rolling.

◊◊◊

The meal was delicious, and the conversation animated. For the first time in months, we laughed, teased each other, and spent a normal evening together.

On the way back to my car, I kick myself for not bringing up our relationship, not wanting to spoil the evening.

Before I can open my mouth, he steers into a quiet pull off, and switches on the interior light.

"Baby, we need to talk."

His serious eyes meet mine. Uh-oh, no good ever comes from '*we need to talk*'.

Preparing myself for the worst, my heart sinking into my stomach, I sit up.

"Okay, what's bothering you?" I try not to let my anxiety creep into my voice and remain calm.

"Helen, I want you to know I'm as serious as a heart attack about you—about us. I'm tired of hiding, want you for my Old Lady, and I'm warning you, I won't accept no for an answer. I've fallen so hard for you, it's difficult to breathe. You're it for me, Helen. I love you, warts and all."

It feels like I have been struck on the head with a baseball bat. All those words I so carefully prepared fly out of the window. He loves me? Holy hell!

After taking a moment to collect myself, I reach for the seat belt buckle and free myself.

"Please, darlin', don't leave me. I'll drive you to your car, but don't get out and walk away from me."

The fallen expression on his face threatens to break my heart. I scoot across the bench and climb on his lap, straddling him, the steering wheel squashing us together. I take his face in my hands and lower my lips to his, happiness and desperation tainting the kiss.

Licking the seam of his lips, he opens for me, and I slip my tongue inside, stroking his, deepening the kiss, until we are both breathless and panting.

"I won't leave you, you fool." I smile at him.

"I love you too, so much, and I'd be the proudest woman on earth to be your Old Lady. You'll have a hard time getting rid of me." I giggle.

"Otis, I've loved you from the first moment. It just took me a while to realize. You make me so happy, and even in the hardest times, your love shines a light into the darkness." I snuggle myself even closer against him, heat flaring between us.

My pussy is dripping, and I need him. I grind myself against his hard cock, trying to gain friction, giving my throbbing clit some much needed relief, but he lifts me up and plonks me on the bench next to him.

"Helen, you are driving me insane. The next time I take you it's going to be in a bed, not in this SUV like a horny teenager. You deserve better than that."

"You better follow me home then and make good on that promise." I pout and swat his thigh as he bursts out laughing.

"Not funny," I whine.

"Oh, baby, I have no qualms taking you home, putting you in my bed, and making sure you don't leave for days. I'll worship you all night"—he waggles his eyebrows at me—"but there is the slight issue of the Club to discuss."

There, that does it. My libido deflates instantly.

"I honestly don't give a wet fart about the Club. Whatever it is, they'll deal with it."

"Yes, but have you thought about Tanya and Pennywise? How they'll take it?"

"Otis, I know they aren't in a good place, but that doesn't mean we can't be happy. We cannot keep putting everyone else before us. We have a right to be happy, to be with each other. Everyone else be damned. Knowing my son, he'll be happy for us. I'd hope Tanya will be the same. I know she's struggling right now. But I get your concern and want to spare her as much as possible.

"Saying that, I'm sick and tired of hiding, too. I don't want to replace her mother, nor would I want you to replace Pen's father. But we can work as a blended adult family."

Masher stares at me, his eyes dark with need.

"God, woman, I'm so hot for you right now. I love your no-nonsense attitude. Your place or mine?"

"Mine, definitely mine. At least no one will come bursting through the door there. Now put this damn thing in drive and let me pick up my car. You can follow me home." And with that, we're on the road like a flash.

He follows me back to my house. I don't live on the club property. When we had Noah, Bear and I bought a house in town, trying to keep Noah as far away from the then harsh club life as possible. We wanted to give him a home. Since then, I've remodeled it twice. It's my cozy bolt-hole, with a soundproof music room for my sax, guitar, and my drum kit.

As I open the door, I lean in to switch the alarm off, including the monitoring system Ferret installed at the beginning of the year when Rusty became a problem. There are cameras hidden in every room, but they only work once the monitoring system is live—usually when I'm out, or at the Clubhouse taking care of my family.

I switch on the lights and watch Masher as he walks past me into the short hallway.

"Want the tour?" I ask him.

"Sure, show me the coffee maker first, so I can make you a cup in the morning." He bats his eyelashes at me, making me giggle like a schoolgirl.

"Okay, this is the kitchen." Switching the light on, I walk to the fridge, swaying my hips on purpose. I know he's staring at my ass.

Taking out two beers, I hand one to him.

"This is the Keurig." I point toward the corner of the worktop. "Cups and everything you need are in the cupboard above it." I smile sweetly at him.

I lead the way on. "This is the living room. The door to the left houses my music room. Out back there's the yard, with a hot-tub, and the gate leads to the garage we parked in. No direct entrance into the house from the garage, I'm afraid. Now if you'll follow me," I say in my best realtor impression, "upstairs are three bedrooms; the master has an en-suite and there's a family bathroom." I point to the two spare bedroom doors and the bathroom door.

"This is the master," I just manage to squeak out, as suddenly I'm hanging upside down over Masher's shoulder, and the next thing I know I'm in the air, then bouncing on the mattress, as he throws me onto the bed.

"Wow, not bad for an old guy," I tease.

His eyes are on fire.

"Four-poster, huh, oh the things I could do with you, making use of all this bed offers," he growls.

"Promises, promises," I croon, standing up, unbuttoning my blouse, taking it off, and showing off my lacy, see-through bra. I struggle to hold in my laughter as I turn to switch on the bedside light, and all I can hear behind me is his boots hitting the floor and him hopping, trying to get his clothes off as fast as humanly possible. I shed my jeans and stand before him in just my sexy underwear.

"Let me," I tell him, pushing him down onto the bed, unbuttoning his shirt slowly, and running my hands across his broad, hair-speckled chest. I love running my hands through it.

I lean down and kiss him, unhurried and tender, then sink to my knees and let my lips follow where my hands have been, trailing kisses all over his chest and torso. Resting back on my thighs, I free his legs from his tangled jeans, pulling them off, taking his socks with them. On the way back up, I start kissing his inner thighs up one way and down another.

"Baby, you're killing me here," he groans.

My hands reach for his boxers, and I stroke his length through them, making him hiss. I pull on the waistband, and he lifts his hips, so I can slide them down, his hard cock jutting up proud against his stomach. I lick my lips, eager to taste him, but he lifts me up off the floor.

"Not that I'm not enjoying you on your knees in front of me, but it's my turn now."

3 — MASHER

Within a nanosecond, I've swapped our places and fall to my knees in front of my woman. My cock is so hard, I think it'll fall off if I don't get inside her soft heat soon.

I pick up her dainty foot, kissing every toe, her musk permeating my nose, driving me insane with need. Her whimpers only spur me on. Nipping, licking, and kissing my way all the way up the inside of her long legs, I hit the apex and work my way down the other side.

"Quit messing around, man. I need you inside me, now," she grumbles at me.

"Easy, tiger, you've had your fun. This is my show now." Good job she can't see the grin splitting my face.

In response, I grab hold of her legs and yank her down the bed, so her glorious pussy hovers over the edge. Her little squeal fuels my desire.

I attack her clit, sucking it hard into my mouth, and she bows off the bed, groaning.

"Yes, honey, right there."

She's writhing in pleasure, and instead of giving her what she wants, I lick my tongue straight through her saturated folds. She's dripping for me. The need to really taste her is overwhelming, and I bury my tongue inside her, sucking up her nectar while fucking her like this. Every moan leads me onwards.

"Baby, you taste so fucking good. I'll never get enough," I groan, inserting one finger into her tight heat, then two, while my tongue gives her hard nub some attention. I curl my finger and reach for that magic spot, and she goes off like a rocket. My rocket.

Before she's come all the way down, I flip her over, position myself at her scolding entrance, and push in with one hard shove, until I bottom out.

Then, I pause for a beat to give her time to adjust. After three months, maybe I should have been a bit more careful.

"Jesus fuck, Masher, you feel so good when you fill me like this, but please move, I need you to move. Fuck me, big man, like you mean it!"

I don't need to be told twice. Withdrawing until only the tip of my leaking, aching shaft remains, before I slowly fill her again, to the hilt. Her pussy flutters around me and my control snaps. I hammer into her again and again. My balls are boiling and the tingle at the base of my spine lets me know I gotta make her come before I shoot my load and coat her insides.

Reaching around, I stroke through her folds, wetting my finger in her arousal, before I press it to her clit and rub in hard circles. With a scream, her walls contract, strangling my dick, and I can't hold back, exploding deep inside her with a shout of my own. Our combined juices drip out of her, running down my balls. I don't mind if she paints me as much as I painted her. I love the feel of us together.

Boneless, she collapses onto the bed. My now softening member slips out of her.

I walk to the bathroom, find a washcloth, wet it with warm water, and move back to the bed, proceeding to clean my woman, giving her the care she deserves.

After throwing the cloth in the hamper, I climb into bed, pull the blankets over us, wrap my arm around her, and pull her back into my chest. I know it sounds ridiculous, coming from a man like me, but I love spooning my Old Lady. Nuzzling her neck, stroking her sides, her contented sighs are music to my ears.

"How was your day?" She turns around, facing me, her hands running over my back, relaxing me instantly.

"Okay, I guess, same shit, different day at the moment. I'm working at the garage with Sparks, Ratchet, and the others. Nothing new from the Slayers, so all is calm. Raven's been a shit, though. He palmed organizing a Christmas party off on me. Tree, presents, the lot. I've no idea where to even start."

Even I can hear that I'm complaining like a little bitch, and Helen is biting her lips so hard, she'll make them bleed.

"Go on," I sigh, "laugh all you want. I can take it."

"Not laughing," she says, trying and failing to cover her cute little snigger.

"Want me to help you? It's only four weeks until Christmas, so you'll be stretched for time doing it all on your own," she offers, and right now I could kiss her silly for it.

"Helen, please, I beg you, your help would be invaluable."

"Ah, but what do I get in return?" Minx.

"A lifetime of orgasms and bragging rights?" I hope she goes for this, but she's devious, so all bets are off.

"Okay, that will do."

Huh, that was easy. So why am I worried?

"Love you, baby, not just because you're helping me out. I just love every bit of you. The good, the bad, the gorgeous, and the ugly." No sooner has the word left my mouth I realize I could kick my own ass. I didn't mean it like that.

"The ugly, huh? Aren't you lucky that I haven't got a vindictive bone in my gorgeous body?"

Oh shit, I'm up the creek without a paddle or canoe in sight. I sigh. Might as well just take it like a man. I mean, how bad could it be?

Helen turns around, and I draw her into me again. I listen to her breathing until it evens out. Just in case I snore, I want her to fall asleep first, before I finally close my eyes and drift off.

◊◊◊

Groaning, I turn my alarm off. One of the guys must have gotten a hold of my cell and set the alarm to a rooster's crow. Sometimes I feel like I've entered the twilight zone. I take a second to realize I'm in Helen's bed, not my own. She's still fast asleep, so I sneak out of bed ninja-style, head to the bathroom, do my business, take a quick shower, and get dressed.

Closing the bedroom door gently, so not to wake Helen, I traipse down the stairs. First thing: coffee.

After setting the Keurig in motion, I open the fridge and retrieve the fixings for bacon, eggs, and pancakes. After my third cup of life-giving nectar, I set a tray with breakfast and coffee for Helen and carry it upstairs.

"Hey sweetheart, time to wake up," I whisper in her ear.

She stretches like a cat before she opens her eyes.

"Hm, that smells good. I could get used to this." She smiles at me, shuffles up, and sits against the headboard. Once I've placed the tray on her lap, I walk around, set my cup on the nightstand, and sit on the bed next to her. Enjoying the peace, we sit in amicable silence while Helen devours her food. Once she's done, she places the tray on her nightstand and turns to me.

"I had an idea about the Christmas party. I think we should keep it a family get together rather than a club party. Have a Christmas tree, and plan a nice, traditional Christmas dinner. Turkey, glazed ham, cranberry sauce, all the trimmings. What do you think?"

"I think my mouth's watering at the mere thought of it," I agree.

"The club has been through a lot in the last year. It'll be nice for everyone to have a breather and the chance to relax. Can I leave the dinner plans to you? I'm talking to Raven today to see what the budget is. Then we can sit down and plan this shindig." I nod at her, smiling, not quite believing my luck. Being in the same room as her is all I want for Christmas. Everything else is just fluff.

Determined to show her my gratitude, I kiss her thoroughly, even though it makes me hard as steel. Then, I get up, grab the tray and my cup, and leave her to get up and ready. Carrying everything down to the kitchen, I load the dishwasher. I'm nothing if not domesticated.

Her footsteps alert me to her presence. She steps up to me, drapes her arms around me, and lays her head on my chest.

"Are you going to tell Raven what's going on between us?"

"Yes, baby, I want to claim you at the table at the next meeting, so I'll have to put him in the picture. Why?"

"Should we maybe speak to Tanya and Pennywise first? I'd feel better if Pen didn't find out at the meeting, but from us." She looks uncertain, but I have to agree.

"Helen, I think you're right. Not sure how I didn't think of it myself." Kissing her fingers, I realize I want to put my ring on it, as well as my cut on her back.

"Let's go over to theirs this afternoon, get it over with," I suggest.

Helen goes onto her tiptoes, smacks a kiss on my lips, nods and says, "Okay then, let's go, big guy, or you'll be late."

She grabs her keys from the sideboard, throws them to me, opens the door, and lets me exit first. I don't like it, but it makes sense, since I don't know the alarm code. I walk to the garage, back out the car, and pull it up in front of the house. Getting out, I open her door for her and help her inside, before closing her door. Jogging round the car, I get in and drive towards the Clubhouse.

Of course, Caleb stares at us as we arrive together. In fact, his eyes just about pop out of his head. I guess we'll have to hurry putting everyone in the picture before the bush drums do the job for us.

Reversing Helen's car into her spot, I hurry around, hold her door open for her, and watch her sway her delectable ass as she walks away toward the Clubhouse doors.

Plucking my cell out of my pocket, I dial.

"Hi, Dad, are you okay?" Tanya's voice comes through the speaker.

"Yes, I'm fine, darlin'. Just wondering if I can pop over after work? Be nice to catch up."

I cross my fingers behind my back, hoping she doesn't pepper me with questions.

"Sure, you're always welcome. You know that, right?"

"Sure do. Oh, and don't worry about feeding me, I'll bring pizza," I tell her.

"Great, see you later then, about six?"

"Okay, sweetheart. See you then."

"Oi, lazy ass, get your backside in here, there's work waiting to be done!" Sparks' shouts across from the garage are met with my middle finger, as I turn to go see Raven.

4 — HELEN

My thoughts race as I walk into the kitchen. What a night! My legs are still weak, and I feel every deliciously sore muscle after the workout Masher gave me. After three months, I'd almost forgotten what he feels like when he takes me hard. I love his gentle side, but in bed, I almost prefer his roughness.

I take in the sight before me. It's obvious that we left late, as chaos reigns supreme. Since Vegas, Raven, Slender, and Dawg have moved into houses, the girls are no longer here to help with breakfast. Dirty pans and dishes stack up a mile high in the sink, and I'm sure the only place my cast iron frying pan is fit for is the garbage can. Don't think there is any saving it. What on earth did they do this morning? A bacon-and-egg competition of who can burn the thickest layer in the pan? Slobs! The lot of them. With a sigh, I roll up my sleeves. There's nothing for it, but to get started, especially if I want the kitchen in a usable state before dinnertime.

As I start to sort out the mess, my mind whirrs. I noticed how Caleb stared at the two of us in surprise this morning. Not that he's a blabbermouth, but best get ahead of the curve, I suppose. Abandoning the dishes, I wander out of the kitchen on the hunt for my son.

After hunting high and low, I finally find him in Ferret's office.

"Hey, Mom, what's up?" he asks as Ferret gives me a chin lift, as though I'm one of the boys.

Returning it, I take a deep breath. "Noah, can I have a moment of your time? There's something I want to talk to you about."

The fact alone that I called him by his given name makes him sit up.

"Of course. Can it wait half an hour? We're in the middle of something. I'll come and find you when we're done here, okay?"

"Sure, Son, no problem. I'll be in the kitchen on cleanup duty."

Glaring at Ferret, I ask, "What the hell happened in there? The place looks like a bomb went off right in the middle of it."

At least he has the good grace to look at his shoes, his expression like a naughty child getting chewed up.

Letting him stew, I huff, turn on my heal, and leave, pulling the door behind me with a loud click and snickering to myself. Ferret is one of my favorites. Calm, collected, army-shaped. Though you can tell that his time in the Marines and serving in both Iraq and Afghanistan has left deep scars within him.

The next half hour I spend scrubbing and cussing the boys out under my breath.

When I hear the door open behind me, I throw the cloth in the now-clean sink, grab two cups, and pour coffee, fixing Noah's the way he likes it, before turning and handing it to him, pointing at the table.

"How's Tanya?" I start.

He hangs his head before looking up at me, as though it's a really difficult thing to do.

"She's sad but coping better."

"Oh, Son, that's good to hear." I smile at him.

"I've suggested maybe some counseling, but she doesn't want to know. She feels she's coping well enough with everything the last year threw at her. Let's face it, being shot was only one of the things she's had to work through."

The droop of his shoulders tells me all I need to know. He worries about her. Their love is strong. Tanya, although extroverted on the outside, is very much introverted when it comes to her feelings and needs. I tried to suggest getting help, but it only got me my head bitten off. So now, I try to let her come to me if she needs me.

"How are you doing? Anything I can do to help? You know, you've just got to ask, Noah."

"I'm getting by, Mom." He sighs. "Anyway, what's up, Mom, what did you want to talk to me about?"

"Noah, there's no other way to tell you this, so I'll be straight up. I'm seeing someone. Have been for almost a year now, off and on, and we want to make it permanent. He loves me and I love him; he makes me happy."

A huge smile splits Noah's handsome face almost in half, joy radiating from him. This is the son I know and love.

"Mom, that's great! I know you loved Dad, but it's been a long time, and I want to see you happy. I'm stoked!" He jumps up, comes round the table, and wraps me in a bear hug, squeezing so tight, I have trouble breathing.

Well, that went better than I thought.

"Don't you wanna know who it is?"

"I don't care, as long as you're happy, Mom. You can tell him from me though, if he hurts you, he's a dead man walking!"

Deep breaths, Helen, deep breaths.

"You can tell him yourself; Masher is in the garage working."

"What did you say? Did you just tell me you're with Masher?" If I didn't know better, I'd say Noah's eyes are about to pop out of his head.

"Didn't think you were hard of hearing, Son. You need me to clean them for you?"

"Masher? Seriously?"

"Yes, Masher. You got a problem with that?"

"No, not at all. He's a good man. I'm just surprised. You kept that quiet, didn't you? I don't like that you kept this from me."

"Noah, with all due respect, I am a grown woman; I know what I'm doing and don't need to justify myself to anyone. We took a break to be there for you and Tan. You needed us more. Now you are getting on, we are doing the same. He asked me last night to be his Old Lady, and I accepted. I just wanted to give you a heads-up, since Caleb saw us drive in together this morning."

"Mom, I have no problem with you and Masher. I'm glad you found someone who makes you happy. The fact he asked you to be his Old Lady makes me breathe easier. He's serious about you. I'm grateful for all you two have done. But, as you said, life moves on, whether or not we like it, and I'm stoked for both of you."

"How do you think Tanya is going to take it?" The thought of loading more onto her plate worries me.

"I'm sure she'll be happy too." Noah smiles at me. I get up and refresh our coffees, and we sit there chatting for a while, before he stands and puts his empty cup into the dishwasher.

"Right, Mom, I have to go. Tanya has a check-up appointment at the hospital, so I'm taking her.

"Okay, Son. We'll come over this evening to speak to you both together, so I'll see you later." I hug him to me, kissing his cheek, and watch him grin, turn, and walk away.

The rest of the day goes by in a flash. Cooking dinner for the hordes—my homemade lasagna—takes a lot of my time. So do the memories of last night.

The terrified look Masher gave me after his little faux pas.

"I just love every bit of you. The good, the bad, the gorgeous, and the ugly."

I love him to distraction, but I think a lesson is due to be taught. The ugly. I'll give him the ugly.

The kitchen door flies open, and Raven struts in with Chloe under his arm.

"Hey, Mom, Masher spoke to me about the Christmas plans. I think Christmas dinner is a great idea. How much do you need? No, scratch that. Consider yourself to have an unlimited budget. Use the housekeeping credit card as you see fit. I've given Masher his budget, so all is good." He smiles at me.

Chloe steps out and wraps me in a hug. "Congratulations," she whispers in my ear.

That answers whether Masher spoke to Raven.

"Thank you," I whisper back, watching Raven grin and shake his head at us.

"Chloe, can I borrow you for a bit?" I think I'm going to need support if I want to put my plan for an unforgettable Christmas for Masher in motion. No time like the present.

"Sure, Mom, I've got a few hours before Raven is done here. What do you need?"

"Well." I wink at her. "It's like this…"

5 — MASHER

Knocking on the door, I wait until I hear Raven shout, "Come in!"

I step into his office and am surprised to find him reclining in his seat with his feet on the desk.

"What can I do for you?"

"I want to take an Old Lady. Since it's got to go through a vote, I came to you first, so it can go on the next Church agenda." I'm trying to sound normal but am quaking in my boots.

"Oh? I didn't realize you're seeing someone." His eyebrows raise up to his hairline, not helping my nerves in the slightest.

"Been seeing her for almost a year but took a bit of a break these last three months, concentrating on Tan, you know. Last night we talked and are making it permanent. She's agreed to be my Old Lady."

"So, when are we going to meet the woman who puts up with your sorry ass? No one has seen you with a woman since you joined us, as far as I know."

"You might not have seen us together, we kept a low profile, but you know her." Taking a deep breath, I prepare myself for the ass chewing I expect. "Helen and I have been kinda hiding it. First because of the two different clubs issue, then family matters—"

"Hang on a minute here," Raven interrupts me. "Helen? As in Mom? Are you out of your goddamn mind? You can't be serious. She's Pennywise's mother! All the brothers' mother for that matter."

"Raven, I'm deadly serious. I love that woman with everything I've got. She's brought peace into my life when I least expected it. There's nothing I wouldn't do for her."

"I'm glad to hear that, since if you hurt her, you won't just have Pennywise to deal with, but the entire Club will bay for your blood."

"I'm aware. Since I've no intentions of hurting her, I can live with that."

"On your head be it. I have no objections; you both deserve happiness. I'll put it up for the vote next meeting. Congratulations, you old goat."

With a huge grin, he gets up and claps me on the shoulder, so hard I almost topple over, much to his amusement. His chortles follow me out of the room.

Shit, I forgot the budget. Turning on my heels, I step back into the office.

"Back so soon? Changed your mind? Do I have to give you a beatdown?"

Man, Raven can be really irritating.

"No, I forgot to ask you about the Christmas budget. I discussed it with Helen last night. She feels, rather than a full-on party, we ought to make it a family get together, with a traditional Christmas dinner, a tree, presents, just a nice, traditional celebration."

"Not a bad idea." Raven strokes his beard, deep in thought.

"I'll speak to Mom about it in a bit. I can separate out both your budgets. Will a grand do you?"

"I sure hope so. Can't cost that much to get a tree and some decorations," I reply.

"You'd be surprised. If you need more, we get the brothers to chip in. Now fuck off and get to work." He winks at me, pointing at the door.

Saluting, I walk out of his office and blow out a relieved breath. That wasn't too bad.

The rest of my morning is full of ribbing and hard work. Seems like every Duluthian wants their car serviced or fixed before Christmas. Not that I mind, but my thoughts are not on the job. After snapping off the third wheel nut of the morning, I throw my wrench in the corner in disgust. Fucking oaf.

"Maybe they should have called you Nut Buster." I roll my eyes; Ratchet has to throw in his two cents. The man can't seem to help himself.

I pick up my torque wrench and go after the little shit. Christ, he's fast.

"Maybe they should have called you whippet," I wheeze after three rounds of the garage.

"You're doing it wrong." Sparks smirks, sticking out his foot as Ratchet runs past, sending him flying across the shop floor.

"Ah, you little bastard, that hurt!" Ratchet gets up off the floor and limps back to his station.

"Poor little whippet. Want me to call you an ambulance? Or maybe Chloe can stick a Band-Aid on for you?" Sparks teases.

"Fuck off, asshole!"

I'm just glad the focus is off me.

◊◊◊

Thank God today is almost over. I've washed up and am now heading to the kitchen, where Helen's dishing up lasagna for the boys. I've ordered pizza for us to take to Pen and Tan's and am just waiting for her to finish up.

"Boys, if I ever find my kitchen in a state like this morning again, I'll open up a castration center. I'm sure Chloe would help. Once one of you does my job—cooking for all of you—you can leave the kitchen however you like. In the meantime, you are all capable of tidying up after yourselves and loading the dishwasher; you aren't children. Be warned. Once more, and I'm going on strike!"

Helen is on a roll. I'm taking note not to piss her off. She's fierce! I'd hate to get on her wrong side.

"Come on, let's go. These reprobates can manage on their own," she says and points to the door.

Nodding, I let her take the lead and follow her to her car. It's not far to Pen and Tan's house; it's on the property, but it's cold out, and I'm sure Helen prefers to be able to leave directly, without having to walk back to the Clubhouse.

Just as we walk into the parking lot, the Prospect jogs up with our pizzas and hands them over.

Helen gets into the car, relegating me to the passenger seat. As I slide in, she starts the engine and guns it. I've never grabbed so tight onto the *oh shit* handle in all my life. I think she believes she's a Redbull stunt driver! That woman strikes the fear of God into me!

Once we arrive at Tanya's, I get out, bending over with my hands on my knees, gasping in air, thanking the Almighty for letting me live this time.

When I straighten up, Helen is staring at me, hand on cocked hip.

"Something you want to say?"

"No, dear, must have been something I ate for lunch," I reply, knowing better than to admit of being scared shitless by her driving. I don't want to sink myself any deeper into the hole I dug for myself last night.

Wrapping her in my arms instead, I press a hard kiss to her lips. I love how she softens against me.

"Ewww, gross!" Tanya shouts from the now open door; then, she spins on her heel and slams it in our faces.

"So much for telling them gently." Helen shrugs, grabs my hand, and drags me up the stairs onto the porch. Once she's opened the door, she drags me into Pen and Tanya's, pizzas squashed, but still perfectly edible.

Tanya looks at me like Helen just did outside, but fiercer and with both hands on her hips. Honestly? My daughter scares me sometimes.

"So, you have a dirty little secret." She frowns at both of us. "How long has this been going on?"

"Oh, about a year," Helen answers, grinning at Tanya, while Pennywise is hanging over the couch, head down, trying to suppress his laughter.

"A year?"

Lordy, my daughter can screech with the best of them. I cover my ears, but Helen just grins at her.

"Sorry, darlin', we would have told you earlier, but, you know, the time just never seemed right. We made it official last night, so we're telling you now."

"What he said," Helen chimes in.

"Daddy, you are such an idiot," Tanya rails on me, while walking over to Helen and pulling her into a tight embrace.

"Congratulations, Helen, or can I call you Mom now? Let me warn you, he's a blithering idiot half the time, and needs a tight rein. Thank you for taking him off my hands." With that she kisses Helen's cheek, a bright smile and mischief light her face, reaching her eyes. I fight the tears welling up, and looking at Pennywise, I catch him wiping his sleeve over his eyes with a big grin on his face.

I'm so relieved that Tanya has taken things so well, but when Pennywise pipes up, "Please, can I call you Daddy now?" I groan, turn, and bang my head repeatedly against the wall.

"You lot will put me in an early grave, I swear. No, you may not call me Daddy, nor Father or Father-in-Law. Not happening. Have you lost your goddamn mind?"

I don't mind making a fool of myself. Tanya's laughter is a balm to my soul.

"Give me that pizza, you heathen," my daughter not only commands, but rips the squished boxes out of my hands.

She and Helen disappear into the kitchen, and in no time, plates and cutlery are clinking and cluttering on the dining table.

"How did the doctor's appointment go?" I keep my voice as low as possible as I question Pennywise. He replies likewise.

"We got an official apology from the hospital director after the complaint we made. They'd like to settle with us, since we threatened with legal action."

"Good, so they should, Pen. Their treatment was abysmal, to say the very least," I grouse.

"We had a long talk about it on the way back, but I'll let Tanya fill you in. We better get in there before they organize a world war between them," he snorts out.

I couldn't agree more.

6 — HELEN

"Hey, girl, how are you doing now?" I ask Tanya, glad she took our news so well.

"Better, Mom, a little better. The way they treated me during my last stay still makes my blood boil, but they also offered counseling, which I agreed to. It helped that their contracted counselor is Darcy, and that I can schedule sessions with her directly at Debs' Haven."

I pull Tanya into a tight hug.

"I'm so proud of you, girl. Hey, if you feel up to it, would you like to meet with me and Chloe tomorrow? She's helping me plan a *unique* Christmas celebration. You could join us. It'd be great to have you on board." I wink at her.

"Mom, you are the second most devious person in this house, right after me, so yeah, I'll join you. Time to socialize again. When and where?"

I give her the info just as Masher and Pennywise enter, grab beers out of Tanya's fridge, and hand them out before we sit and eat in amicable silence.

As we finish, Tanya leans forward, elbows on the table. "You know I said about the hospital appointment, Mom? Well, that wasn't all."

"The hospital director turned up and apologized to us officially. You know we put a complaint in and threatened to take them to court? Well, they want to settle out of court with us. How much for I don't know yet, but I've decided whatever money they'll pay, will go to charitable causes. What do you think?"

"Oh, love, I think it's a brilliant idea. I'm sure we can get the Club to help as well, to bump up the funds if need be. Maybe have a Secret Santa for Christmas presents, and the boys put an equal amount of what they spend in a big piggy bank. What do you think?"

"Fab idea, Mom," Pennywise interjects. "I was only planning on spending twenty dollars on a present for Tanya, means a cheap Christmas for me."

Whack!

"Ouch." Pennywise rubs the back of his head.

"Twenty measly dollars? On my daughter? You better come up with something better than that, or else!"

"Yeah, yeah," my son grumbles, "I know, she'll kick my ass."

"Too right, with my steel toe boots!" Tanya glares at him before giggling.

"Right, time to go for us. Don't want to be late again," Masher says, pushing back in his chair.

"Yeah well, we wouldn't have been late, had you let me sleep last night," I answer.

"Lalalalala, not hearing this…" I laugh at my son, sticking his fingers in his ears, squishing his eyes shut tight.

"Come on, Old Man, I know when we're not wanted." I snigger, grab Masher's hand, and pull him up.

"See what I got to put up with?" he mocks

"Self-inflicted, now deal with it," Tanya replies.

◊◊◊

Back at home, we sit down on the couch, snuggled up, drinking a last cup of coffee.

"Well, baby, that went better than expected." Masher sighs. "Don't know what I was so worried about. Good to see Tanya perky, too."

"Yes, it was. I'm so glad she's picking up a little," I agree.

"I spoke to Raven today, since Caleb saw us. He's happy and bringing it to the table at the next meeting. Can't wait for you to wear my cut, and only my cut." He winks at me.

I sit up and straddle him.

"Well, Old Man, are you going to take your Old Lady to bed and show her what you're made of?" I whisper in his ear.

"Your wish is my command." With that, he stands. I close my legs tight around his waist and squeal with laughter as he carries me up the stairs and into the bedroom, where he pushes me firmly against the wall and kisses me long, deep and hard. Not laughing now…

I groan as he presses his impressive, hard dick straight into my crotch, setting my clit on fire. I rip at his clothes, pulling his T-shirt over his head. My hands go for the top button on his jeans, while he rips off my blouse, sending the buttons flying like tiny projectiles, tinkling as they hit the floor. I lift my arms to help him, watching the blouse land on the floor behind him. He doesn't bother undoing my bra; he pulls the cups down instead and makes short work of feasting on my aching breasts. My nipples pebble so hard, it's almost painful, and a zing goes straight to my clit, drenching me.

"I love your tits, so soft and delicious," he growls in my ear as he nips the lobe.

I struggle to get his jeans open, but manage to pull them down his hips, freeing his bouncing cock. He rips down my leggings, pushes my panties to the side, and unceremoniously buries himself in me to the hilt in one brutal stroke, filling my soaking pussy so deeply.

Throwing my head back onto the wall, I groan and soak up the sensations, which border on pain as he stretches me. It only makes me hotter. I don't have to ask him to move. He hammers into me, truly fucking me to within an inch of my life, and I take it. Take it all and love it all.

"Harder, honey," I encourage him, and he's not shy in obliging, pounding into me like a machine.

I can feel myself tensing, reaching for the release, but not there yet. He changes the angle, and oh my God, he now hits my clit on every stroke. That's all it takes.

"Masher!" I scream, before biting his shoulder in all-consuming pleasure, as wave after wave of contractions, release, and bliss roll over me.

"Oh fuck!" He groans as he empties himself inside me, filling me with his cum.

Once we've steadied our breathing, he gently puts my feet on the floor.

"Wow, that was..." For the first time in my life, I'm lost for words.

"Exactly," is all he sighs out.

Getting undressed almost seems like an afterthought, but we do, before we hop in the shower together, complete our nighttime routines, and finally crawl into bed.

I snuggle my back into him, soaking up his heat, taking in the scent of his body wash, feeling content.

"Love you, Helen," he whispers in my ear.

"Love you too, honey," I mumble before sleep pulls me under.

◊◊◊

Ugh, I've been up since five a.m.

Masher snores like a damn warthog! I got up before I gave into temptation and kicked him in the balls. He must have smelled the bacon, as he ambles down the stairs, rounds the counter to reach me, and presses a kiss to my cheek.

"Morning, baby. Did you sleep well?"

"No, did you?" I smile sweetly.

"Yes, fantastic, honey, thank you."

"You're lucky to be alive," I hiss at him. "You've been snoring like a damn chainsaw all night. You're lucky I love you or else you'd have woken up with no balls." I sneer while shoving bacon and eggs on his plate, before slamming the plate on the kitchen counter, and watching as he winces.

"Sorry, baby, I only snore when I'm overtired. You must have taken it out of me last night."

"Well, we better not have sex again then," I snip, knowing full well I'm being unfair. I'm not a morning person at the best of times.

We eat our breakfast in silence and drive over to the Clubhouse straight after.

"Sorry, I don't mean to be grouchy," I mumble as I wrap my arms around him to kiss him goodbye for the day.

"It's okay, baby, I've got broad shoulders, I can take it. At least I now know you're not good with early mornings."

I nod while snuggling into his chest.

"See you later, baby," he croons as he muzzles my ear, before kissing me tenderly, then turning and walking toward the garage.

When I enter the kitchen, I realize my hissy fit yesterday has worked wonders. Everything is tidy and spick-and-span; even the dishwasher is running. So I make myself a cup of coffee. I need at least three of those before I feel human.

Just then the door opens, and Chloe and Tanya step in, grab mugs, and fix their own life-saving nectar.

"Okay, ladies, let's plan." I smirk, pulling a notepad and pen out of a cabinet drawer.

"Let's settle dinner first," Tanya says.

"Okay, suggestions please." I look at both of them.

"Turkey, glazed ham, slow-roast lamb for meats," Tanya suggests, and I nod. Sounds good.

"Roast potatoes, biscuits, gravy, mash, green bean casserole, honey roast carrots, and mixed vegetables," Chloe adds. I agree and it goes on the list.

"Homemade cranberry sauce, mint sauce for the lamb, and I want to try a British recipe of Brussel sprouts in butter with bacon. For dessert I'm thinking pumpkin pie, apple pie, fruit cake, chocolate cake, and warm chocolate brownies with ice cream," I add. "What do you think?" I look between the two of them.

"I think," says Chloe, "that Ally can bring the fruitcake and chocolate cake from the bakery, same with the apple and the pumpkin pie. All we need to do with those is stick them in the oven to warm up."

Nodding, I make a list and allocate those bakery items to Ally.

"My mouth is watering just thinking about it," Tanya groans. "I've not had Christmas dinner in years. I volunteer for making the brownies," she adds, and I mark her down for it.

"Now then, girls, I already mentioned to Chloe that I plan on making Christmas special this year. Tell me, does anyone in the club, apart from myself and Pennywise, play an instrument?"

"Ally plays guitar, I think," Chloe replies. "Caleb's a drummer, and I think Chris plays bass, though I'm not certain. I think he was jamming with Caleb the other day," she continues.

I take notes and try hard to keep the evil smirk off my face.

7 — MASHER

You'd think organizing a Christmas party was easy, especially in a biker club, with all the facilities on hand, but hell no, it's not.

The hours I spent with Caleb, trailing through Dollar Tree, Target, and any other shop you can name, I'll never get back. I'm not a chick. I don't have the faintest idea what to get. So, we piled ornaments, lights, garlands, these gnomes Tanya told me are in fashion, even an oversized elf on the shelf in the cart until the wheels started squealing, and the lady cashier had to open another checkout, so others could pay for their purchases.

Now the chicks have come up with wanting Santa legs and a red sack poking out of the bottom of the huge open fire in the Clubhouse.

So, off I went and got a large Santa—couldn't find just Santa's legs—and a big red sack, stuffed full of newspaper.

They asked for scented candles too, but I drew a hard line there. They want scented candles, they can get them themselves.

Just under two weeks to go, and most of the decorations are up. Everything looks good, even if I say so myself.

I knock on the office door and wait until I hear Raven shout, "Enter!"

"Raven, can I borrow the Prospect later today?"

"Nope, you had him for days. If you didn't get everything done, tough luck. I've given him a list of jobs I need him to do. You'll just have to do without him."

"The women want the fireplace working, so they can light it on Christmas Day. When was it last swept?" I ask, fearing the answer.

"No idea, Masher. I don't believe we've ever used it. It'll need checking," Raven replies.

"Do we have the equipment?"

"Yes, I think there is a rod, brush, and ball somewhere in the bunker. Tell you what, I'll get Caleb to get it for you when he's finished with his other jobs."

"Thanks, Raven, appreciate it."

Next on my list: giving Helen a hand with one of her secret projects.

She's waiting at the bar for me.

"What took you so long?"

"Quit bitching, woman, I'm here now. What do you need help with?"

"Follow me," she says, winking at me.

We traipse through the parking lot, up the path, past the bunker, and I wonder if she's sending me on a fool's errand. We reach a coppice of trees, and hidden within is a shed. Helen pulls a key out of her pocket, opens the padlock, and smirks at me.

"Surprise!"

My eyes bulge out of their sockets.

In front of me is a full-blown moonshine factory. Glass jars with screw tops as far as the eye can see. Shelves and shelves of the stuff.

"Are you shitting me? You did that? How long have you been at it?" My mind boggles.

"Oh, a few years. Some of it is plain, some flavored. There's peach, strawberry, pine needle, apple pie, salted caramel, and Christmas pudding flavor, all double distilled. Wanna try?"

"Does a bear shit in the woods? Of course I want to try."

She hands me a jar labeled pine needle. Seriously? Pine needle? I look at her doubtfully but open the jar anyway. The aroma of woods, pine, and Christmas assaults me. Smells like one of them scented candles she loves so much. I take a deep breath, preparing myself, and then take a small sip. Man, it burns as it goes down, but once the burn wears off, the amazing taste explodes in my mouth. This stuff is good. Fantastic in fact.

“Wow, babe, this is amazing! You could sell it, you know?”

“It’ll come in handy for the Christmas party. Now grab one of them crates over there and fill it with a selection of everything. I’ll keep it in the pantry for now. At least I know it’s there then.”

We both grab a crate each and load up. She makes me drag the crates outside before she locks up and disappears behind the shed, only to return with a wheelbarrow. We load the crates in the barrow; I push it back to the Clubhouse and carry them into the pantry for her.

“Hey, babe, I forgot to tell you, we have Church tonight, so do you mind if I take you home and use your car to get back here?”

“I was wondering when you were gonna tell me. Pennywise mentioned it earlier, but sure, no problem. I’ve fixed a load of sandwiches, fried chicken, biscuits, gravy, and a shed load of chips for dinner for the boys, so if you like, you can take me home now.” Helen smiles, turns on her heel, grabs her coat, and walks out the door ahead of me, throwing the keys over her shoulder.

Just as we walk into the parking lot, Caleb comes rushing towards us, carrying the chimney cleaning tools.

“I’ll leave them by the fire for you,” he announces, gives Helen a little wave, and disappears around the corner.

Dang, Raven was serious. I have to do it myself.

◊◊◊

"Silence, assholes, let's get this done!" Raven bangs the gavel, getting our attention.

Immediately, the chatter and ribbing stops.

"Agenda points for tonight," Raven starts. "Business reports, Dawg needs support, Restless Slayers update, and Spen is here to make a proposal." Everyone cheers. Spen has been away for months, clearing his head after the death of his wife and Old Lady.

"Settle down," Raven bellows. "Next are Prospects, Old Ladies, and any other business."

"Dawg, you're up."

"Okay, assholes, businesses are doing great. Zippy's is pulling in more dough than we expected. Well done," Dawg states.

"Having the second artist made an enormous difference," Zippy throws in. "She's still apprenticing, but she has her own book now, so she's almost there. Any idea when Tanya is gonna be back? We miss her, and we just haven't got the time to deal with everything. If she's planning on being off longer, could maybe someone else stand in for her?" Zippy's question is more than valid.

"Here's a thought." Dougal looks at Zippy. "Jade is doing great now. She's being homeschooled by Sarah right now and doesn't want to go back to school. Jade is petrified someone will ask her questions she doesn't want to answer. She's just turned fifteen. Could she help you out until Tanya is back? She's very organized and always keen to help."

I can't blame the girl. Being rescued from human trafficking after being held in an underground cage would leave its mark on anyone.

"I'd have to discuss with Eve, but I can't see an issue. When could she start? And what hours could she work?"

"I'll speak to her and Sarah, and I'll let you know." Dougal nods at Zippy.

"All other businesses are doing great. Leather and Lace remains a firm favorite. Financially, we are more than solid," Dawg finishes.

"Now, brothers, I need help. Doing the Treasurer's job and being the Secretary takes up too much of my time. I propose Masher to take over as Treasurer."

The bastard has the cheek to wink at me and blow me a kiss! What the fuck? I'm enjoying being a member and not having the officer responsibility for once.

"I second." Pennywise smirks at me.

"Okay, let's vote."

I glare at Raven, who just grins.

The vote goes round the table and is met with all Ayes.

"Damn it, Raven, I was enjoying the peace." I glower at him. "Since all of you assholes voted, I accept."

Everyone shuffles a chair to the right, and I move to my new seat, with Dawg shoving the books at me.

"We'll go through everything tomorrow, brother. It's all organized, don't worry," he assures. I just grunt at him, rolling my eyes.

The door opens and a riot breaks out as Spen walks in. The noise of fists drumming on the table, feet stomping, whistling and clapping is as deafening as Spen's grin is blinding.

"Spen, how nice of you to join us," Raven ribs him.

He finds an empty chair and sits down.

"Hey, brothers, great to be back, not for long, I hope." He smirks.

"Have at it." Raven nods at him.

"You all know why I went nomad. I've been clearing my head, exploring other areas. Wisconsin in particular. It's a nice place. On my travels, I came across the Dark Skulls MC. A nice bunch of guys, but about to go defunct, as their members either died off, ended up in prison, or don't agree with their current president, who's a stubborn asshole. They want to patch over, sans president. It would mean setting up a new chapter. I'd like to transfer, if you decide to go for it." Stunned silence reigns around the table at Spen's words.

"Now, that I didn't expect," Raven says.

"I suggest, Spen, you meet with Ferret, myself, and the other officers, bring some of theirs, and we have a separate meeting. This is a big proposal, and we need to deliberate it carefully, as it could cause a major ruckus."

"Wouldn't expect anything less," Spen replies.

"I brought some men with me. Left them at Leather and Lace while I'm here."

"Okay, officers' meeting tomorrow morning, and follow-on meeting as a meet and greet to feel them out after that. Does that suit?" Raven asks Spen, who simply nods.

"Right, I'll leave you to it." With that, Spen gets up and walks out, while the brothers look at each other, stunned.

"Let's get back to it," Raven proclaims.

"Prospects. We currently have Greg, Caleb, and Chris. Greg has more than done his time, and Caleb is sound, but does he need longer? Chris, we can patch in after Christmas."

Ratchet raises his hand.

"Caleb's great, he's solid, and I'd like to second him for voting in as a brother, since I'm his sponsor."

"Let's vote then. First Greg to become a brother." The votes go around and are unanimous.

"Same for Caleb," Raven announces. Again, the vote is unanimous.

"Let's get them in."

Vegas gets up and straightens his cut, Pennywise follows suit and with stern faces they leave the room for the bar, where the prospects are getting ready for the meeting to finish.

I suppress a chortle as Vegas and Pennywise stomp back in, dragging the Prospects by the back of their cuts into the room. They are so pale, I'm sure they're shitting themselves.

"What the fuck, Prospects? Are you letting your work slide?" Raven bellows at them.

Without giving them a chance to reply, he continues, in a voice that could shrivel balls in an instant, "I've had reports of your work ethic"—Greg and Caleb fold in on themselves—"and it's been glowing!"

Raven laughs at them, shoving two sets of full patches down the table.

"Get sewing, brothers!"

It's only now that it seems to sink in. Caleb whoops, grabbing the patches, kissing them, and Greg snatches his set off the table, waving them in the air as though they are a winning lottery ticket.

"Patch in party!" Dawg and Slender shout.

"Quiet!" Raven bellows. "Let's get the last bit out of the way." Raven points at me.

"Masher, you're up!"

"I'm claiming Helen. She's agreed to become my Old Lady."

Church is so silent, you could hear a pin drop.

"Okay, let's vote," Raven says. "I'll start. It's aye from me."

The vote goes round the table and is unanimous, though not without ribbing. "Dirty dog," is one of the tamer things thrown at me.

"Masher, since you're now Treasurer, you can order Mom's cut," Raven decrees.

"Meeting closed. Let's party!"

8 — HELEN

My eyes keep searching out the wall clock. Almost midnight, and no sign of Masher. Church usually finishes around nine p.m. at the latest. The road is icy, and I'm worried.

I grab my cell and dial his number, but it goes straight to voicemail. Masher never has his phone switched off.

I debate whether to call Tanya, but don't want to look like a fussing, clingy woman.

Fifteen minutes later, I give in.

Tanya answers on the first ring

"Are you alright?"

"No, Tan, not really. Have you heard from Pennywise? Masher isn't home yet, and his cell is going straight to voicemail."

"Pen hasn't been in touch either. He was gonna catch a lift home with Dad."

"I'll come over to yours, and we'll go and search their route home," Tanya says.

"Thanks, doll, I'm sorry, I just worry."

"Don't apologize, I'm the same. Just don't tell anyone. They'll think I've gone soft."

Ten minutes later, Tanya's car pulls into the drive.

I grab my coat and keys and hurry out the door.

Tanya is furious when I get into the passenger seat.

"What happened?"

"Well, before I drove over to you, I went to the Clubhouse, and you won't believe what I saw," she seethes.

Shit, this can't be good.

"Let's go."

Tanya turns the car into the direction of the Clubhouse and starts driving, frothing at the mouth.

Once we arrive, the first thing I notice is the packed parking lot. Then the loud music spilling out. The assholes are having a party!

Ready to rip Masher's head off, I storm into the Clubhouse, stopping dead at the sight in front of me.

Empty glass jars, strewn all over the place. My glass jars!

Bikers snoring everywhere, dropped where they fell asleep, as drunk as skunks!

"What the fuck?" I hiss out.

"Told ya," Tanya rants.

And there he is. My Old Man, sprawled on a couch, giving his best chainsaw impression, with Vegas hanging over the other arm, head down. Caleb is in a cuddle chair; Tequila, the club girl draped all over him. Greg is asleep on the new pool table, and the rest of them are asleep on the bar, in chairs, or on tables. Slender is the only exception. We find him on the floor behind the bar, pine needle moonshine jar still in hand.

I turn to Tanya.

"You still got stuff up in Pen's cabin?"

She nods. I grab her arm, and we head up the path. She unlocks the door and lets me walk through.

"Any makeup?" I ask.

"Just a few lipsticks I don't wear anymore."

"Let's take a look." I step up to the case she holds out to me, place it on the bed, and rummage through it.

"No wonder you don't wear this," I remark, holding up a bright red, twenty-four hour long-last lipstick, "but this will do the job nicely."

Tanya catches on and grabs a Sharpie and all sorts of other things out of her bag of tricks.

Back down in the Clubhouse, we go to work. Thirty minutes later, we high five each other in satisfaction. Pennywise now sports an indelible ink dick on his forehead; Vegas a no-smudge eyeliner mustache, and everyone else is decorated likewise.

However, Masher now has a red nose, extending across half of his face, and to make sure it stays put, we used setting spray, not once, but four times. He didn't even stir as the mist hit his face.

"I reckon we should set the fire alarm off, see if that wakes them," Tanya suggests, barely keeping it together. "What on earth did they have?"

I snigger. "My very own brand of rocket fuel. I make moonshine, dear, and what they had was double distilled. Tastes great, but man, it'll blow your socks off."

I step into the kitchen, finding the one jar of apple pie flavor left on the previously stacked shelf. Returning to Tanya, I open and hold it out for her. She takes a tiny sip. Her face instantly changes color, followed by a coughing fit.

"Wow, that's potent stuff, but so delicious, once you get over the burn. You got any left?"

"Tons of it, up in my secret lair." I wink at her.

"Good, I want some for Christmas. Pretty please, Mother dear?"

I roar in laughter. No chance any of these idiots will be awake any time soon.

"Let's go home and leave them to sleep it off." I wink at Tanya, walk to the medicine cabinet, and remove all the pain relievers, burying them deep in my pocket.

"Helen, I love you. Not even I would have come up with that." She laughs.

"Let's go back to mine. You can have Masher's side of the bed, and we'll deliver them a breakfast they won't forget in a hurry," I say.

"Hell yes, let's go." Tanya turns and looks over her shoulder, waiting for me to follow. We get in the car, drive home and get a few hours' sleep until the alarm goes off at six in the morning.

The Keurig is already working hard. As I get downstairs into the kitchen, the aroma of freshly brewed coffee permeates the air.

"Thanks, Tanya," I nod at her, "I need this."

"No problem. I love fresh coffee. Nectar of the gods," she replies. We sit at the dining table, enjoying the peace and quiet.

"I wonder whether they're up yet?" Tanya smirks.

"Let me finish my coffee, then we can go and find out." I wink at her.

When we arrive at the Clubhouse, the scene greeting us is not pretty. Few have moved, and the ones who have, only to be sick, sit outside at a picnic table, cradling their heads.

Tanya giggles and slams the door of her car extra hard, leaving a concert of groans in her wake. Everyone else is in the same positions we left them in last night.

We enter the kitchen, start two large pots of coffee, prepare bacon, pancakes, and eggs, and work in amicable silence.

Once we're done, Tanya's devious grin warns me she's about to wake the brothers. She leans down, grabs the largest stock pot in the kitchen and a metal ladle, before walking into the bar.

Even I wince as she bangs the ladle inside the stock pot, like the Devil is after her. I retreat onto the back porch, as the noise level is unbelievable.

Shouts, groans, retching noises, and cusswords are audible all the way out here. That will teach them not to fuck with their Old Ladies. Ally, Chloe, and Ashley must have arrived with Alex, who's screaming his head off.

Then a screech and "What the fuck?" as Sparks' voice reverberates through the bar.

I walk back inside, opening the bar door, and the sight that greets me has me standing stock still. That's before I sink to the floor, crying with laughter. Sparks crawls off the bar, soaking wet, while Ally holds a bucket. The now empty ice bucket.

"That's what you get for being a dirty stop out!" Ally rants at him, her pointer finger nearly taking his eye out.

Chloe stands over Raven, holding a catheter tube in her hand, threatening, "You ever stay out again without letting me know and I'll not use this, instead I'll shove a garden hose up your dick! Got me?"

"Got you." Raven's contrite, rough voice does nothing to ease Chloe's anger. She's pissed.

Ashley, equally furious, shoves Alex at Vegas.

"Here, your son is unhappy, as am I."

She throws the diaper bag at him next.

"You can clean his stinky ass for the next week, and even that might not make up. Couch for you tonight, again." As she rails on him, Vegas stares at her, picks up Alex, and suddenly turns green.

Retching, he carries his son out of the room, holding him in front of him as though he's a bomb about to go off.

"Son, I hate to say this, but man, you stink!"

I stand to my full height and bellow, "Breakfast is ready. You better come and get it before I spit in it!"

One by one they file past me, or should I say shuffle like old men.

"What the hell was in that stuff you put out last night, Masher?"

Masher just looks at me, guilty as a raccoon caught in a trashcan.

"Man," Caleb pipes up. "What a patch in party. Can't remember shit, but hell, I'm glad I'm not a Prospect now. Hate to have to clean up that mess." His smile looks creepy with the bright blue eyeliner beard we drew on him.

Pennywise is the first to notice and starts laughing.

"What?" Caleb sputters.

"Look in the mirror, brother," Pennywise chokes out, tears rolling down his cheek.

Wicked Tanya speaks up. "Wait a sec, I'll help you out." She smiles sweetly as she pulls a compact mirror out of her pocket and hands it to Caleb, who, with a girly screech of horror, starts rubbing his face.

Unfortunately for him, the setting spray did its job.

The mirror quickly makes the rounds. Horrified, Pennywise whips the wipes out of Alex's changing bag and starts scrubbing at the dick on his forehead. His glare at Tanya and tortured exclamation of "What did you do?" is something I'll be telling my great grandbabies about.

Unbeknown to us, Chloe has her phone out and films the chaos that ensues, while the rest of us women are sitting on the floor laughing.

"I can't," Ashley howls. "I'm gonna pee myself."

"If you think I'm changing you too, woman, you are mistaken!" Vegas hollers at her.

Ally is slapping her thighs, tears streaming down her face.

"Oh, ladies, I gotta hand it to you. You are evil geniuses!" Ally coughs out between laughter.

9 — MASHER

Maybe I should have thought twice about breaking into Helen's moonshine stash.

To say that I feel every year of my age, and then some, is not an ample description. There are a bunch of evil little things inside my head, playing darts with the back of my eyeball, while others, I'm certain, are a practicing marching band.

It's day two after the patch in party and I'm still hung over. I'm getting too old for this shit.

Not to mention I'm in the doghouse big time. Helen hasn't spoken to me since the night before last, only handed me a blanket and pillow, so I'm camping on the couch.

We drove to the Clubhouse in loaded silence this morning, so I don't think today is gonna be any better.

The only positive out of that fateful Church meeting is that I now have an office, which I've stocked with a bucketload of water bottles and a coffeemaker. Here I am now, trying to make sense out of the books Dawg handed to me, but the numbers are torturing my brain. Instead of staring at them any longer, I decide to place the order for Helen's cut.

I can't stand another night on the couch. Decision made, I'm taking my sorry ass to the kitchen, where Helen is busy bustling about.

Christmas is only a week away, so she's busy cooking, preparing, freezing, baking, and between all that, she's making sure we're all fed and watered.

I got off easy compared to some. Pennywise still has the dick outline on his forehead and is, like me, sleeping on the couch.

Chloe hid the nail polish remover, so our Prez is still walking around with rainbow nails.

My red nose is still glowing, but thank fuck, slowly fading. If someone else calls me Rudolph, or Frosty, they'll talk to my balled fist. I swear to God.

Entering the kitchen, I walk up behind Helen and wrap her in my arms. She stiffens but doesn't shove me away. Progress.

"Baby, I'm sorry. So sorry. I swear to you, it won't happen again. And I'm extra sorry to have touched your moonshine. That was out of order. I'll take the barrow later and restock what we drank. I swear on my life, I'll not be that stupid again. Being a man, I'm bound to fuck up now and then," I plead with her.

"As long as you've learned your lesson," she admonishes me. At least she's talking to me, so I take it as a small win.

"I promise, no more of where that came from." Leaning in, I gently kiss her neck.

"Fine, you can move back into the bedroom," she declares.

Thank God for that.

"Have you sorted the fireplace yet?"

Shit, I forgot about that.

"No sweetheart, I'll get onto it now." I watch her nod and retreat into the main room.

Moving the pool table by myself is quite a feat, but I manage. Not sure my back will ever be the same, though.

The chimney sweep stuff is where Caleb left it, next to the fireplace. I grunt as I drop to my knees, grab a dustpan and brush, and start sweeping out the fireplace. The dust has me coughing in no time. Making sure I brush off the edges slightly up into the chimneybreast, I'm reasonably satisfied that this bit is clean. Next, I light a firelighter to check whether the chimney actually draws, which surprise, surprise, it doesn't. Good job I used the smokeless variety.

I sigh to myself, grab the brush, and am about to shove it up the chimney, when Dougal comes in.

"Hey, man, want me to go up on the roof and watch for the brush coming out?"

I'm so happy about the offered assistance, I could cry.

"Yeah, brother, that'd be great. Would you mind throwing the ball down after?"

“Sure, no problem. Give me ten minutes though, I’ve got to get the ladder and climb up first.”

I stand and grab a bottle of water from behind the bar; the dust tickles my throat.

I get back on my knees and look up towards the tiny bit of light at the end of the chimney. Surely there should be more light coming through? Though, at least it’s not completely blocked. Best get a tarp to cover the floor.

“You ready?” Dougal shouts down.

“Yes, hang on,” I holler up, grab the brush with the extensions, screw them together, and start shoving them upward to the top.

The first try it doesn’t even go halfway. On the second try I hear Dougal shout, “It’s out!”

I stick my head up the chimney and see that the brush is sticking almost into Dougal’s face.

“Okay, man, I’m pulling back, you can drop the ball, then we do it again,” I holler up, and pull back on the brush, which suddenly speeds towards me like a scalded cat, hitting me on the head, including the ball Dougal dropped. Before I’m able to retreat, an avalanche of soot comes down on me, half burying me in the chimney and fireplace. I try to inhale, but can’t as my mouth fills with soot particles, dancing around me like a snow flurry. I try to crawl back but can’t. Somehow my belt has hooked itself onto the chimney wall.

Fuck, what the hell?

"Sorry, man, the chain slipped through my hand," Dougal yells down, which I almost don't hear, since I'm coughing so much.

"Asshole!" I bellow up.

"What on earth is going on in here?"

At this exact moment, Helen's voice is the last one I want to hear.

"I'm cleaning the chimney," I cough.

"Well, you'll be cleaning the rest of the room when you're done. Why didn't you use the cover?"

Cover? There's a cover?

"Woman, don't wind me up right now. I'm doing your bidding, and now I'm stuck and can't get the fuck out!" I splutter between coughs.

"What was that?" her sweet voice trills from behind me.

"I'm fucking stuck. This soot is everywhere, and I mean *everywhere,* so please, woman, don't be clever. Help me out, please?"

I thought I'd asked nicely, but maybe not, because she answers, "Hang on, honey, let me just call Chloe. This has to go into the Christmas presentation she's preparing!"

Her footsteps fade. I groan and have to listen to her calling Chloe.

Fucking hell, could this day get any worse?

No sooner do I finish my thought process, the steel ball falls through the brush and hits me in my already extremely sore head.

"FUUUCK!" I scream, punching the wall, which loosens more soot, and I'm back in a flurry again, coughing my left lung up.

"Oh dear, what have we here?"

Great! Raven is all I need. Nothing like an audience when things go pear-shaped.

"Raven, I don't care if you're my Prez, one remark on the situation here, and I swear, I'll punch you instead of the wall," I grate.

"Is that so?" He doesn't even bother to hide his laughter.

"How can you be stuck? You turning into a fat fucker?"

Vegas. *Give me strength!*

"My belt is caught somewhere. I can't move!"

Roaring laughter behind me, lets me know it's no longer just a couple of them, but the whole brotherhood.

"Sorry, Masher, I'm short of knives and used my last sheet of sandpaper on Rusty. Must have forgotten to buy more," Dawg joins the heckling.

"Oh, Dad, lucky for you, I came prepared," my daughter cackles.

I've got zero clue what's going on. I'm too busy trying to keep soot out of my mouth and nose.

"Please, Tanya, let me." Helen snickers.

Next, I feel a blade sawing back and forth through my belt and breathe out a sigh of relief when it gives way, and I can finally shimmy out of my precarious situation. In my haste, I forget there's a reason for my belt, and as I stand up to my full height, my jeans hit the floor.

"I hate Christmas and all of you assholes," I gripe, grab the keys out of Helen's outstretched hand, and walk out the door. Hollering and hooting follows me. While I hold my jeans up with my other hand, I open the car door with the other, get in, and floor it out the gates.

10 — HELEN

I'm still chuckling every time I think of Masher and the chimney incident. It was like Comedy Central live from the clubhouse.

With just three days to go until Christmas, preparations have ramped up a notch.

Christmas dinner is almost prepared, only the meats need roasting on the day.

Today, I sent the boys out for a fresh tree. There's a tree farm close by, and to be sure they'll pick a nice one, I persuaded Terrie, Clusseaud's wife, to join them.

She'll make sure they don't return with a dud.

"Hey, Mom," Tanya speaks up from behind me, making me jump about six feet off the floor.

"Jesus, girl, don't sneak up on me like that. You've taken years off my life." My hand grips my chest, where my heart is hammering like a bike engine on crack.

"Sorry, didn't mean to." She titters at me.

"Look, the mailman just dropped this at ours. It's addressed to the club. What shall I do with it?"

"Who's it from?"

"Postmark is from Grand Forks, so it's likely from the Restless Slayers. If it was from Meghan, she would have addressed it to me personally."

"Hm, you better put it on Raven's desk," I suggest.

Masher and I don't talk club business, but I have a bad feeling about this. We've never had a parcel from them before.

Tanya nods and walks off toward the office.

When she returns, it's with a greenish complexion.

"What's wrong?" I'm concerned, and shove a chair under her, making sure she's safe, just in case she passes out on me.

"Emergency Church," Raven bellows from the main room, where most of the brothers and their Old Ladies are congregating, as it's just after business closing hours.

Feet trample through the room and next the Church door slams shut.

"Tanya? What's going on, honey?"

"The parcel. Raven opened it while I was in there with him, in case it was from Meghan. I unwrapped the present. It was a dead, half decomposed rat in a Ziploc bag!" She retches, covers her mouth with her hand, and sprints out onto the back porch, where I hear her emptying the contents of her stomach onto the floor.

Oh, holy crap on a cracker.

Masher storms into the kitchen, face like a revenging devil.

"Where is she?" he growls. I point outside, where I can still hear retching. How he got here this quick, I'll never know, but he beat me to Tanya, that's for certain. I follow him outside to the back porch where he's sitting, with Tanya on his lap, rocking her as though she's still a child. I guess our children will always be our babies, no matter how old.

"Hey, baby girl, it's alright. Shh, it'll be okay." His gentle voice and the way he cradles his daughter, melts my heart. And to my shame, I must admit, it sets my lady bits on fire, too.

I love that soft side of the hard man so much it hurts. I've seen his tough side. Everyone here has. Yet, he has so much capacity for empathy and emotions for the people he loves, it's astounding.

Next thing I know, the kitchen door slams and Pennywise is storming onto the porch. His expression filled with such malice it frightens me.

He lifts Tanya off Masher in short order and growls, "You're needed in Church, I've got this." He plonks himself on the porch, rocking Tanya, whispering in her ear.

I return to the kitchen, fix coffee for them both, and take it out to them. Tanya, slowly calming, accepts the tissue and damp cloth I hand her, to clean her face.

"Thanks, Mom." Her little voice so quiet, it's almost a whisper. I step around my son and wrap my arms around both of them.

"Babe, I have to get back into Church. Stay with Mom until I'm done, yeah?"

"I'll be fine, Pen, you go. I'll help Mom until you come out."

If I get my hands on the dick who sent the parcel, I'll shoot him, no questions asked.

Pen leaves while Tanya and I return to the kitchen, coffee cups still in hand.

"What can I do?" Tan asks me, glassy eyed.

"Tell you what, let's bake sugar cookies. That's about all that's left to do for the Christmas preparations."

"Wow, I haven't done that since I was tiny." Tanya half smiles.

"Let's get you baking then," I encourage, grabbing all the ingredients out of the pantry, scales, and a massive bowl to boot.

We work in tandem. Me mixing, Tanya kneading. I'm glad I'm not the dough under her hands, since she more beats the hell out of it rather than kneads. Who cares though, as long as it makes her feel better.

Grabbing the box of cookie cutters, I open it and tip the contents onto the side.

Suddenly Tanya roars with laughter.

"What?" I'm confused.

"The dick mold," she chortles. "Nothing says Christmas like a dick cookie."

"Girl, you ain't seen nothing yet." I smirk as I continue to shake out the cutters.

There are cutters in every imaginable shape: dicks, butts, boobies, condoms, handcuffs, unicorns, mustaches, and of course more traditional stars, snowmen, Santas, pine trees, and gingerbread men.

"I'll have the boobies and the butts." Tanya howls, making grabby hands. So, I take the dicks, unicorns, and mustaches, and we share the rest.

Both of us cutting makes light work out of the enormous amount of dough. The first lot has just left the oven when Chloe walks in and looks at the baking tray, eyes as round as saucers.

"Please let me help decorate." She claps her hands like a seal.

"Only if you grab us some of that apple pie moonshine, honey." I wink at her.

She opens the cupboard, grabs three mugs, and fills them to the brim with moonshine, as though it's milk. My eyes roll so hard, they must hit the back of my head. After passing the mugs to us, she grabs the icing and starts decorating the still-warm cookies, passing us one each. We all giggle as we stare at the beautifully decorated butts in our hands until Chloe dips hers in the moonshine.

"Eww, disgusting." I shudder, staring at her in disbelief.

"I've had an idea." Tanya's mischievous grin warns us she's up to no good.

"Go on," Chloe encourages.

"We should get an old sock for each of the brothers, give the single ones a couple of condoms each, a tube of chrome polish and a lump of coal. The ones with Old Ladies get the chrome polish and either some perfume or nail polish of the expensive type, since it's for us, plus the lump of coal."

"That's brilliant. I'm just about out of my Chanel," Chloe agrees.

"Maybe we should add an indelible ink pen in each stocking, as a reminder not to mess with us," I add.

Wow, is it warm in here? My face feels so hot, I could fry an egg on it.

As we laugh, decorate, and finish our moonshine, time flies. With all the cookies stored away, we're just chatting when the door opens.

Raven, Pennywise, and Masher step in. Raven stares at Chloe.

"Woman, are you drunk?" He snickers.

"Me? No, not at all! What makes you think that?"

"The open jar of moonshine, and your empty mugs," he deadpans.

"I'm perfectly fine," Chloe protests, gets up, and stumbles over her own feet.

"Yeah, I see that." Raven smirks. "Come on, let's get you home to bed."

“Take me home, you sexy beast!” Chloe hollers, as Raven sweeps her up into his arms and carries her out of the room.

11 — MASHER

We're just loading the tree up when our cells go off.

"Emergency Church," Vegas bellows down the phone.

We throw the tree on, tie it down, jump in the motor, and floor it back to the Clubhouse, and head straight into Church.

My ass hasn't hit the chair fully when Raven hisses, "Message from the Slayers," shoving a box towards me and adding, "Tanya opened it."

With that, I'm on my feet, storming out of Church and into the kitchen, where I last saw Tan before heading for the tree lot.

"Where is she?" I growl at Helen, who points outside. I can hear my daughter retching from here.

Stomping out, I pick up Tanya and sit on the porch with her on my lap, rocking her back and forth.

"Hey, baby girl, it's alright. Shh, it'll be okay." I gentle my voice, trying to soothe her. She's my baby girl, always will be. Anyone hurting her will meet with the barrel of my gun.

The door slams and Pennywise stomps out onto the porch. His face shows the fierce anger I feel.

He lifts Tanya off me, and in short order, growls, "You're needed in Church, I've got this." He plonks himself on the porch, rocking Tanya, and whispering in her ear.

I nod, pivot, and march back into Church.

"How fucking dare they! They brought my little girl up. She was one of theirs. How dare they take their issues with me out on her!" I rant.

"Not just issues with you, man," Raven clarifies.

"I've asked for a meeting to discuss independence from them. After I contacted the big three for their permission, I got it," he explains further. "Seems they don't like that idea much," he adds.

"Regardless, it's a shit stunt to pull," Dawg seethes. "Going after our women is just a big fat no."

"We need a show of strength," Clusseaud barks.

"That we do," Slender agrees, "but not before Christmas."

"We need to keep eyes on our women," Sparks says.

Snickering breaks out, and someone mutters, "Good luck with Ally."

"Settle down," Raven grouses. "I suggest we treat this as a potential threat. Be extra careful, keep your eyes peeled, and try to intercept any mail, just in case they try something similar again. And, Caleb, get this stinking thing off my table," he orders.

Caleb jumps to it, grabs the offending box, wraps the rat back up, and carries it outside.

"We should name him Christmas," Ratchet pipes up. "He's so good at wrapping presents."

"Which would make Greg, Stitch. Since he almost ended up with cross stitches when he was shot," Zippy chortles.

"Ha, ha, hilarious," Greg wines.

"Hey, I heard that," Caleb, sorry, Christmas mutters as he comes back in.

"What, don't like it? Shame. We do, Christmas," Striker winds him up.

"Back to business," Raven admonishes. "You realize this could be a declaration of war?"

He looks each of us in the eyes before he continues, "I propose we prepare. Not only for war, but to patch over the Wisconsin Club to bolster numbers. Ferret has looked into them, and they seem okay. We're meeting with them tomorrow, so we'll report back tomorrow evening. Sorry to ruin your Christmas Eve, but we'll meet again at seven tomorrow. Meeting adjourned. Go home. Pennywise, Slender, Vegas, Ferret, my office at ten a.m."

Raven bangs the gavel, and Church empties into the bar, where Tequila and Clarity are on duty. Clarity is a new girl, a friend of Ebony's, and popular with the single guys.

I follow Raven and Pennywise into the kitchen. We find three red-faced, giggling women sat at the table, plus an empty jar of moonshine and three empty mugs.

Raven stares at Chloe.

"Woman, are you drunk?" He snickers.

"Me? No, not at all! What makes you think that?"

"The open jar of moonshine, and your empty mugs," he deadpans.

"I'm perfectly fine," Chloe protests, gets up, and stumbles over her own feet.

"Yeah, I see that." Raven smirks. "Come on, let's get you home to bed."

"Take me home, you sexy beast!" Chloe hollers as Raven sweeps her up into his arms and carries her out of the room.

This reminds me exactly why I patched over. The love, the laughter, and the occasional Action Stations.

"Hey, asshole, let me down, I can walk!" Tanya gripes as Pen picks her up, throws her over his shoulder, and carries her out.

Helen stares me down. "Don't you dare, caveman!"

"Caveman, huh? I'll show you caveman," I warn her, before I grab her and follow Pen's example by carrying her out to her car. Once there, I unceremoniously plonk her into the passenger seat. Thankfully, the giggles set in as I stoop and buckle her in.

She giggles the entire way home. And yes, home is what it feels like now.

The looks she shoots me from underneath lowered lashes, man, there's fire in her eyes. My woman is horny as hell, it seems.

Her hand wandering across my thigh, squeezing and kneading it, tells me more than words could. It's when she unbuckles her seat belt, though, that I'm realizing I better pull over.

Before I can find a pull off, she's turned to me, her hands on my jeans, opening button after button. My dick, which has been hard since we left the clubhouse, is having a dance behind my fly, knowing it's gonna get some action, right here, right now.

"Hells, stop right there. I'm driving, babe. I'll take care of you once we get home, I promise."

"Nope." She grins mischievously at me, her hand wandering into my pants.

The soft warmth of her skin makes me hiss and my cock pulse. I want to squeeze my eyes shut but I must keep them peeled on the icy road. I groan as she pulls me out of my boxers, the warm air hitting my throbbing head does nothing to calm me.

Where's a pull off when a man needs it?

My thoughts jumble as the sensation of her velvety soft hand rhythmically stroking me up and down takes over.

"Helen, you gotta stop," I groan, trying my hardest not to close my eyes as she works me.

Oh, thank God, a pull off.

I hang a right, brakes catching hard, putting the car into a brief slide, before coming to a sudden stop.

My seat belt is off within a nanosecond, and my head hits the headrest as the scent of her perfume mixed with arousal hits my nose. I wish I could bottle the aroma filling the car and my nostrils. It's a heady mixture. Not to mention how it has my need for her spiraling, the sensations overwhelming.

"Hells, please stop," I implore. "I need to come inside you, need you so bad, but I'm not making love to you in the backseat of a car like a high schooler."

Her eyes hit mine, a soft smile playing across her lips.

"Shh, big man, I love you, all of you, just where we are. I need to show you just how much. Let me, please? All you need to do is sit back and relax," she whispers, and her declaration of her love has me capitulating instantly.

She takes my face in her hands and turns it towards her, her gentle caress causing a bolt of electricity to shoot through me, her tender, feather-soft touch almost more than I can bear. Animalistic need races through my veins like an unstoppable freight train heading for a collision, setting my whole body on fire. It's taking everything I have not to lift her up and impale her on my dick.

When she leans in, placing a soft kiss on my lips, her tongue softly licking at the seam of mine, I open for her. The taste of sweet moonshine and everything that is her makes my already pounding heart beat into a frenzy. Her tongue strokes mine, filling every inch of me with her delicious taste, driving me insane.

The loss of her lips on mine when she pulls back feels like sweet torture.

Before I can open my eyes, a shout leaves me, as her soft tongue hits the head of my throbbing dick, licking up the pearls of precum that have gathered there, spurred on by her ministrations.

My balls are churning, and when her soft, hot mouth closes around the head of my cock, sucking and licking as though it's the sweetest lollipop she's ever tasted, I know I'm done for.

Panting and listening to her soft groans vibrating across my dick, almost makes me lose it there and then. Reciting the Declaration of Independence, imagining my grandma in her underwear, I think of anything to try to stave off my impending explosion. Though, the tingle at the base of my spine is sending my brain haywire.

"Hells, please, slow down, babe. I won't last."

Her answering groan sends more vibrations over my already hypersensitive flesh.

All I want to do is rip her mouth off my dick, shred her clothes into ribbons, and fuck her into next week, but she's relentless.

When she finally lifts her mouth off me and smiles, I think this might be my chance, but a beat later she lowers her mouth back onto me, relaxing her throat, and taking me so deep I feel the back of it enveloping me like a glove. Then she swallows around me and I'm a goner.

Flashes run across my vision as she rides up all the way to the tip of my dick, licks the head then goes down on me again, swallowing, repeating her ministrations again and again, until I can't think straight. My eyes are crossed, and the burning, broiling in my balls becomes unbearable.

"Hells, you need to stop. I can't hold off anymore," I beg, only to be rewarded with a deep hum around my dick.

Her next deep swallow sends me over the edge. My cock twitches as though electricity has been shot through it, and I spurt ream after ream of cum down her throat, seeing stars flash across my vision. And my woman just swallows and swallows every drop of what I give her, like she's thirsty for it.

Once she's licked me clean, she leans over, smiling, kissing me deeply. The taste of myself and moonshine combined sends my senses into overdrive all over again, and in an instant I'm so hard again, I could pound nails.

This woman will be the death of me.

12 — HELEN

I might be a little drunk and I know I frequently rail on him, but I love Masher with everything I have. My feelings for him run so deep that I'm questioning whether Bear was ever my it. I loved Bear, there's no mistake about that, otherwise I wouldn't have married him and had Pennywise, but the intensity of feelings coursing through my veins for Masher are on an entirely different level.

Despite being older, at fifty-five, I feel like a young woman when I'm around him, and in my head I'm still twenty-one.

The physical and emotional need for Masher sometimes frightens me a little. Until I realize how lucky I am, having found love not once, but twice in my life. That, and probably the moonshine, inspired me to show him exactly how much I love and want him.

Especially after how hard I've been on him since we got together.

Going down on a man isn't generally my favorite thing, but tonight I was so desperate for his taste; I threw all caution overboard.

"Masher, I love you so much, so all-encompassing, it scares me sometimes." My voice is barely above a whisper, I doubt he's even heard me, but there, I admitted it.

"Babe, I feel the same." He looks at me while driving us back home. "You mean everything to me. Helen, I cannot imagine even a second of my life without you. You drive me nuts in all the best ways."

Soul-deep happiness suffuses me with warmth until I could burst, and my eyes sting at the sweetness of his declaration.

The car stops outside our garage and Masher turns to me.

"Hells, you drive me crazy. Now get that fine ass of yours out of this car and inside so I can fuck you, make love to you, and then fuck you again."

My already soaked vajayjay releases another rush of moisture, pooling between my legs, and I can't get out of this damn car quick enough.

I race to the door, through it, turn the alarm off, and strip. By the time Masher joins me, my clothes are off, until only my lace panties remain, and I'm ready to attack him, his taste lingering on my tongue.

Like a hunter stalking his prey, he moves towards me. His eyes almost black with desire.

I groan and rub my thighs together. The scent of my arousal obvious to both of us.

His hand goes to the buttons of his jeans. My eyes, mesmerized, track the progress of his fingers as each button pops open. He steps closer until his breath strokes my face. Then, he grabs my shoulders and walks us backwards until my butt hits the back of the couch.

"Hmm," he draws in a breath through his nose. "You smell so delicious when you're hot for me. The mix of your amazing perfume and your wet pussy turns me on like nothing else. I love your pussy wet, more for me to suck and lave up. Best dessert ever."

His dirty words only take me higher, climbing the incline to release.

Without words, he turns me around, pushes my upper body over the side of the couch, pulls my soaked lace panties to the side, and pushes in, in one long hard stroke until he's seated to the hilt.

Pleasure ignites inside me, shooting sparks throughout my pelvis, making my clit throb unbearably. His stilling, to give me a moment to adjust to his rather impressive size, draws a whimper from me.

"Please, honey, move, I need you to move," I beg.

His control snaps, and he hammers into me in short, sharp, deep thrusts, hitting my cervix every time, driving me insane with the need to come. The suede of the couch rubbing my nipples sends constant zings to my clit.

"Harder," I plead, squeaking in surprise when he lifts my hips, changing the angle. Each thrust now hitting my Gspot makes me cry out. My brain being utterly fried has my thoughts narrow to a pinprick, the only reality being my overwhelming need for release.

When it comes, it hits like a bomb, making me see stars, with tears pouring down my face. His name leaves my lips with a cry, and him groaning as he pulses inside me, releasing his hot cum, making me feel every spurt, prolongs my intense orgasm until I think I might pass out.

His body covers mine, both of us panting hard, as we slowly drift back down from the amazing high we just reached together.

When he lifts himself off my body, I mourn his loss, as his now softening cock slips out of me.

"Stay there," he tells me.

His footsteps move away, only to return almost immediately. I sigh as a warm damp cloth hits my sensitive parts and he tenderly cleans me, wiping the evidence of our mixed fluids away from me. For such a big man, he's incredibly tender.

Masher turns me around, grabs behind my knees, lifts me up, and carries me upstairs to our bedroom bridal-style. All I can do is lay my head on his shoulder and try not to cry with the incredible feeling of love, happiness, and pleasurable exhaustion filling every part of me.

My heart, my body, my soul.

He undresses both of us, my limbs too boneless to help to strip my panties. Then, he pulls the blanket over me as he lays me on our bed. The mattress dips under his large body as he climbs in and pulls me close. Snuggled into him, his warmth and breath on my skin, I'm lulled to sleep within minutes of hitting the bed. His safe heat resolving all my thoughts, wiping away all the questions I had. All that can wait until morning.

◊◊◊

The room is still bathed in darkness when I wake. Lifting my cell from my nightstand, I groan, noting it's only six a.m. Way too early for Christmas Eve morning and way too early to get up. When I turn around, Masher's smiling eyes greet me.

"Morning, sweetheart," he rasps, voice still rough from sleep and his hair all mussed.

"Morning, darling, did you sleep well?" I kiss his cheek, aware of my morning breath.

"Like a baby. Stay in bed, babe; I'll make us coffee and bring it up, we can talk then. I need to bring you up to speed with a few things from the meeting." He kisses my cheek and throws back his side of the blanket. I stretch, nod at him, and wait until the bedroom door closes behind him.

No sooner has he left the room, I jump out of bed, deal with my business, brush my teeth, and jump back into bed. I'm amazed that I'm hangover free. The moonshine hit me last night, but there are no lasting effects, not even the teeniest sign of a headache.

I only opened it because after that lovely present shocked all of us, we needed something to fortify us, since worry marred all our faces.

Masher returns with two steaming mugs in his hands. The aroma of freshly brewed coffee, making me reach out.

“Gimme, gimme, gimme!”

Masher laughs at my pleading whine.

“Here you go, sweetheart.” He holds one mug towards me.

I take a sip and shudder, my face contorting.

“What’s wrong?” he asks, his body stiffening, on full alert.

“Toothpaste and coffee are not a brilliant combination.” I shrug.

He sets his mug down, laughter making his taut, muscular, and very naked body shake. He’s in fantastic shape for his age, and I have to close my mouth to stop drooling. All I need to do is look at him and my ovaries are doing a happy dance.

He climbs back into bed and sits against the headboard, sipping his coffee.

“Hells, the Slayers are pissed. It looks like they’re spoiling for confrontation,” he starts. “That stunt they pulled yesterday. It’s likely only the beginning.”

“Should I be worried?” I ask.

“Maybe. Maybe not. It’s too early to tell, but in any case, please be extremely vigilant when you’re out and about, and don't go out without a brother with you. I'm not trying to clip your wings, Helen, I'm just trying to keep you safe."

"I know, babe. I promise I'll be on my best behavior, and make sure I'm carrying as well. If any of them fuckers come near me, I'll shoot before I ask questions. I'm fed up with their shit," I grouse.

I take another sip of my coffee and an idea hits me.

"Hey, I have band practice in three hours. Want to join me?" I ask, praying he won't. It would make things very awkward.

"No, sweetheart, I can't. Need to get the accounts done. Raven wants to look at them after Christmas, and I'm only just getting my head around them. But I'll make a call," he promises, looking contrite. Little does he know he's doing me a big favor by not coming along. I almost feel a tad guilty.

Masher picks up his cell.

"Morning, Christmas," he says.

What the fuck? Who is Christmas?

"Could you be over here at ten? Helen has band practice, and I need to sort the accounts. Thanks, man, I owe you one. Yes, put the tree up. I'm sure we can all pitch in to decorate. Sure, see you in a couple of hours."

"Who the hell is Christmas?"

Masher laughs.

"It's Caleb. In Church, he showed us he's a hotshot at wrapping presents, hence Christmas."

I shake my head at the childishness of the brothers but can't suppress my chuckle.

"Hey, Helen, I nearly forgot to mention, we have another meeting tonight at seven. Do you mind coming with me? I don't want you alone in the house. Not until we know what's going on with the Slayers."

"Sure, no problem. I can get the girls together and we'll finish the last preparations for tomorrow. Including decorating the tree." I smile at him.

We spend the next couple of hours doing our own thing; him going through accounts, and me going through kitchen stock lists, sharing the office downstairs. It feels cozy and domesticated, which is a new one for us.

At ten o'clock on the dot, Caleb arrives, and we head into town.

13 — MASHER

I spend hours poring over the accounts. They are all in perfect order. Dawg did a brilliant job with them, but looking at them in more detail, I can see why he needed help. Being Treasurer is plenty of work on its own, never mind if you hold down the Secretary position as well.

When three p.m. comes around, I close the books, grab the keys, my cut, and get into the car.

With the windshield frozen solid, I start the old girl up, get out, and scrape the windows.

By the time I'm done, the heater kicks in. I squeeze my tall frame into the driver's seat, swearing for the hundredth time about how small the space is. Straight after Christmas, I'll buy Helen a new car, preferably a truck, giving her a bit of added safety, and me a bit of comfort when I have to use a cage. With my cut folded neatly on the passenger seat, I put the car in drive and head out towards the clubhouse.

As I enter the bar, I'm greeted by brothers gathered openmouthed around the Christmas tree. I stop dead as I spot what they are staring at. The top of the tree is a mangled mess. Oh shit, Helen's gonna kill me.

"What the fuck happened to the tree?" I growl.

As one, they all turn, pointing at Stitch.

"What did you do?" I round on him.

"Sorry, Masher, I pulled the garage truck up, didn't see the tree, and ran right over it." At least he has the decency to look red-faced and shameful.

"You buffoon!" I yell, advancing at him, ready to knock his teeth out.

Stitch legs it away from me and a chase around the butchered tree ensues, until Vegas puts a stop to it by grabbing Stitch at the back of his cut, effectively toppling him over.

Slender grabs me around the waist, pulling me away.

"Calm down, it was an accident," he sneers at me.

"Accident? You tell Helen that, 'cause I sure as shit don't fancy having my balls cut off," I rail at him, making him wince.

"Come on, boys," Raven orders. "Let's get this tree sorted out, before Helen gets back!"

Huh, I'd like to see how they're planning on fixing this. Its crown is gone, only a gaping hole where the treetop once was. The trunk is split in the middle, making it lean like the tower of Pisa halfway up.

"Sparks, Ratchet, see what you can find in the garage to fix this up." Raven nods towards them. They hurry out.

"Dawg, Dougal, any ideas?" Raven raises a questioning eyebrow at them.

"Let's saw the frayed bits off the top for starters," Dougal suggests.

Dawg meanders off, in search of a saw, I guess.

Sparks and Ratchet return.

"Here, Clusseaud, come hold the trunk this side. Zippy, you take the other side," Ratchet says, waving an exhaust repair bandage and a roll of duct tape around.

Zippy and Clusseaud get in position, pushing the split trunk as far back together as possible, while Sparks wets and uses the exhaust bandage, wrapping it around tightly, to stabilize the trunk. Then Ratchet uses the duct tape to keep it all in place until the bandage hardens out. *This might just work.*

Dawg returns with a handsaw and climbs the stepladder Dougal steadies for him. Wobbling like a drunk on the top of a tree, he takes off the split center. I've got to admit, it looks a little tidier, but it's still a sorry excuse for a Christmas tree.

"Looks like a pity tree," Striker jokes.

"A what?" Halfpint asks.

"A tree someone takes pity on because no fucker else would put it up in their house. Could be a new tradition," Striker mocks.

"Yes, and out of pity, we'll stick all you assholes underneath it," Raven heckles. "Since we're all here, let's do Church early, then see if we can pacify Mom."

Instead of answering, everyone turns, walking towards the meeting room.

“Okay, so we met with the rest of the Wisconsin guys this morning,” Raven starts. “Ferret checked them all out. Gotta say, Spen did a good job, he had all their details in a file ready for Ferret last night, and Ferret worked through the lot. They all seem legit.”

“Not only that, but they are keen. They’ve had a run in with the Slayers before, so are happy to support us, should it come to an outright war,” Vegas adds.

“There’s ten of them,” Slender continues. “They have voted in their officers and are ready to go as soon as we give them the okay. Spen will be their Treasurer and Secretary, just as he was here. Their Prez is called Grizzly, VP is Shadow, SAA is Digger, and their Enforcer is Bones. Most of them are ex-military, and they have one established business in security. They’ll take over the Clubhouse they already have; they’ve already ousted the old Prez. Grizzly used to be their VP, so is used to leading.”

“Has anyone any concerns or questions?” Raven asks, looking at each of us in turn. “Let me make it perfectly clear. If we patch them over into a new chapter, making us the mother chapter, the Slayers will be on the warpath, for sure. We need to vote as well on independence. We’ve got the three large national clubs’ permission, but I don’t want to push this on you.”

Raven waits for a beat and since no one has anything to say, he starts off the voting.

“Okay, first vote for the Stormy Souls MC to become independent. I vote Aye.”

The vote goes around the table, and even Moggy votes Aye, so it’s unanimous, and Dawg enters the vote into the journal.

“Second vote,” Raven says. “For the Wisconsin club to be patched over and from now on be known as the Stormy Souls MC Madison Chapter WI. I vote Aye.”

Raven opens the vote, which once again goes around the table and is unanimous.

Raven pulls out his cell and dials.

“Grizzly, Raven here. We voted. Welcome to the Stormy Souls.”

Raven pulls the phone away from his ear and grimaces as loud hollering and cheering rings through the speaker.

“Grizzly, bring your men over after Christmas, and we’ll have a patch over party. Yes, New Year’s Eve is great. We have more than enough room for you. We can talk more then, hold a joint meeting. Yeah, agreed. Okay, party hard, and tell Spen to get off his ass and order your new colors. I expect to see them on New Year’s Eve.” Raven grins and ends the call.

“Any other business?” Raven asks. “No? Meeting closed.”

He bangs the gavel on the table, and we all file out. The animated chatter dies instantly when we see Helen, Chloe,

Ashley, Sarah, Caroline, Terrie, and Ally standing in front of the Christmas tree, hands on hips, jaws hanging open.

"Oh shit," Vegas mutters, trying to sneak out of the door.

"And where do you think you're going Mr. VP?" Ashley thunders, stopping Vegas dead in his tracks.

"Raven, what the hell is this supposed to be?" Chloe spits.

Helen just looks at me. If looks could kill, I'd be a shriveled pile of ash at her feet.

"Sparks, you poor excuse of a biker, if you want to hide something, don't use exhaust bandage and duct tape," Ally jeers.

We all groan in unison. Damn, that went over like… I'm lacking an adequate comparison.

"Well done, Dad, you picked a gorgeous tree," Tanya mocks.

"The tree was fine, treetop and all, when I left it yesterday," I complain.

Finally, Stitch steps up.

"It was me, ladies. Sorry, I backed the van over it. My sincere apologies."

"Was it now?" Helen turns and takes a step towards him.

Stitch turns on his heels and runs out the Clubhouse like his ass is on fire, rather than facing her wrath.

"Good to know I haven't lost my touch." She cackles like a witch on Halloween.

"Come on then, boys, let's make this ugly duckling pretty," she says, pointing at the boxes and boxes of decorations.

Tanya is bringing in trays of eggnog, and we all laugh and clown around while decorating the tree.

"Let's have a lock in, since we're all drinking," Vegas suggests.

The idea gets taken up with loud cheers of agreement and we all relax. The only one who isn't relaxed is me. I'm searching out Tanya.

"Do you have it?"

"Yes, Dad, and I followed your instructions to the letter. I'll bring it tomorrow morning."

She's as calm as a cucumber, while I'm shitting a brick.

14 — HELEN

It takes ages, but we manage to hide most of the tree's imperfections under the decorations. Apart from the treetop. Instead of the angel sitting on top of the tree, it slouches in a hollow at the top, surrounded by lights.

We all head to bed rather merry, and I fall asleep as soon as my head hits the pillow. Not even Masher snoring wakes me up.

When morning arrives, I wake and have to re-orientate myself. We're in Masher's old cabin, rather than our house.

It's Christmas morning, and the thought alone fills me with warmth and excitement for the first time in years.

I sneak out of bed, leaving Masher to sleep and make the first coffee of the day. It's only seven a.m., but I have to make Christmas breakfast, as well as starting Christmas dinner. The turkey is pre-basted but will take hours to cook.

I pad into the bathroom, take a shower, get dressed, and wake Masher with a kiss and a mug of freshly brewed coffee.

"Morning, sweetheart," he grumbles. "Is that coffee I smell?"

"It is, my love. You stay in bed. I'm going down to the kitchen," I say and stroke his stubbled cheek.

"Merry Christmas, sweetheart." Masher sits up in bed, leans forward and wraps me into his arms, kissing the top of my head.

"Merry Christmas to you too, honey." I snuggle into his arms for a moment and let him hold me to him, enjoying the feel of his body and his warmth.

Getting up, I walk to the window and draw back the curtains.

"Oh look, Masher, it's snowing!"

A slow falling, but thick flurry of snowflakes silently creates a winter wonderland outside.

Masher chuckles.

"I love seeing you this happy," he says. "That's the best Christmas present I could ask for."

My heart warms at his words. Before I can change my mind, crawl back into bed and devour him, I smile and walk to the door.

"See you soon, honey." I blow him a kiss and close the door behind me.

As I make my way through the freshly falling snow, I smile to myself, holding out my hand, catching flakes and watching them melt in my open palm.

I use the back door to the kitchen, and as soon as I open it, the aroma of freshly brewed coffee assaults my senses.

Ashley, Ally, Tanya, and Chloe are already around the table, with a mug left out on the side for me.

"Mom, I've got the stockings in the car, even labeled them." Ally grins.

Tanya hands a small package to me.

"Thanks, darling, for wrapping it too."

Tanya kept my present for Masher safe for me. I didn't want him to stumble across it. It took me ages to find the right present, and I don't want to spoil the surprise.

"No problem, Mom, he's gonna love it." She smiles at me.

Ally gets up and retrieves the stockings from her car. Well, socks, but who cares?

We pin them onto the wood paneling by the fireplace. The fireplace itself isn't big enough to hold them all. We giggle, staring at the misshapen socks dangling, admiring our handiwork.

Then we get to work on breakfast. Bacon, eggs, sausages, potato cakes, pancakes, baked beans, tomatoes, mushrooms, maple syrup, blueberries, oatmeal, and cereals all fill the table to bursting. The turkey goes in the oven; the lamb and ham are prepared and ready to go. Potatoes are peeled and pre-boiled, the only thing left for the dinner is peeling the sprouts, cooking them with bacon and frying them in butter, but I'll do that later.

Chloe goes up to wake Raven; Ashley does the same for Vegas, who's on Alex duty this morning, and Tanya volunteers to knock on every chalet and door to get everyone else up.

I start up the stereo system in the Clubhouse, find a Christmas song playlist, and add my Bluetooth speaker, which I take into the kitchen.

One by one, the brothers appear and settle around the laden breakfast table. It's wonderful to see all of my family together like this. We even take time to say grace before we all dig in. The kitchen, full of warmth, love, and laughter, is my happy place. After breakfast, the boys insist on tidying away and loading the dishwasher and send us out into the main room with coffee and a tin of my homemade biscuits.

Terrie and Clusseaud arrive, all smiles and very late, not minding having missed breakfast. Even Ebony, Tequila, and Clarity join us, which is unusual for the club girls, who normally stay well away from Old Ladies.

I get up and hand them a present each.

"Merry Christmas, girls."

"Thanks, Helen, you shouldn't have." Ebony smiles at me while unwrapping her present.

I bought them each a bottle of their favorite perfume and chocolates. They each come and hug me, Clarity with tears in her eyes.

"Thank you so much, Helen, it's the first present I've received in a long time."

"You're welcome, dear," I reply, thinking that maybe we judge the club girls too harshly. Every one of them has their own story.

Slowly, the guys trickle in. Pennywise is the first to notice the sock parade.

"What the hell, brothers? It looks like Santa has been here."

He might be smiling now, but wait until he opens his stocking.

The guys can't wait to pull them off the wall.

The single guys start howling with laughter as they empty theirs. A pack of condoms, an apple, and a lump of coal.

Vegas is next to open his. An apple, a pacifier for Alex, perfume for Ashley, and a lump of coal. He groans, but hands the perfume and pacifier over with a grin, bites into the apple and throws the lump of coal into the fireplace.

The others follow suit, apart from Sparks who complains and ends up getting head-slapped by Ally. By the end, we have a nice pile of coal for the fire tonight.

We all continue to exchange presents, and I hand Masher his.

He unwraps it carefully, peeling the sticky tape off with single-minded determination. He gasps when he opens the box.

"Hells, this is amazing," he stutters, holding up his custom Oak and Oscar watch, with motorcycles replacing the hands. It took me months to find. He jumps to his feet, pulls me up, wraps me in his arms, and swings me around.

Laughter bubbles out of me, and to see him this happy, makes me happy. Best present ever.

He puts me down and walks behind the bar, bringing out a massive box. At least thirty inches long. I gape at him as he hands it to me.

Taking a seat, I unwrap and lift off the lid, only to find another box, marginally smaller than the first one. I catch him wink at Tanya, and I wag my finger at her. Hearing her pealing laughter makes the unwrapping worth it. I get to work, and surprise, surprise, I find another box. And another, and another. Halfway through, I find my new cut with *Property of Masher* on the back.

Watching Masher's happy and prideful expression as I put it on makes everything worthwhile. I throw my arms around him, kissing him soundly, and continue unwrapping this blasted parcel.

By the time I'm three quarters through, everyone else has finished, and Alex is asleep in his bassinet. After box number six, I'm losing the will to live, but I carry on regardless, as all eyes are on me.

What seems like hours later, I'm left with a small box, mountains of paper and empty boxes beside me.

"Masher, if that's another box, I'll slap you into next week," I whine, to everyone's tittering.

I unwrap the last box and lift the lid. A small jewelry box falls into my hand. I gasp. When I look up, Masher is on one knee in front of me and you could hear a pin drop.

"Helen, you have brought joy and love back into my life, when I didn't believe I deserved, nor would ever have it. I love you with all that I am, now and forever, and I want to ride with only you on the back of my bike for the rest of our lives. Will you do me the incredible honor and marry me?"

He takes the box from me and opens it. The most beautiful baguette cut diamond ring glitters on a cushion of blue velvet. My hands go to my mouth and my eyes fill with tears.

"Yes, Masher, I'll marry you. I love you so much, you make me so happy. I can't wait to become your wife and ride into the sunset with you. Now, get up off the floor before your knees give out."

He gets up, pulls me into his arms, and kisses the hell out of me. If he wasn't holding me so tight, I would be wobbling, because my knees have turned to jelly.

When we finally come up for air, we're met with roaring laughter and shouts of congratulations all around us

This is the happiest day of my life.

15 — MASHER

My poor heart nearly stopped when Helen finally found the ring box. She was stunned, and without her noticing at first, I went down on one knee. My practiced speech flew straight out of my head, so when she looked at me, I spoke from the heart.

"Helen, you have brought joy and love back into my life, when I didn't believe I deserved, nor ever have it. I love you with all that I am, now and forever, and want to ride with only you on the back of my bike for the rest of our lives. Will you do me the incredible honor and marry me?"

I take the box from her and open it. The most beautiful baguette cut diamond ring glitters on a cushion of blue velvet. Tanya helped me choose it. Helen's hands go to her mouth, and her eyes fill with tears. *Shit, why is she crying?*

"Yes, Masher, I'll marry you. I love you so much, you make me so happy. I can't wait to become your wife and ride into the sunset with you. Now get up off the floor before your knees give out."

I do as I'm told, pull her to me and kiss her like my life depends on it. And it does.

We spend the rest of the time until dinner with our family. Not all of them are blood, but family we choose, for better or worse, and we love all of them.

To say dinner was spectacular isn't doing it justice. We all stuff ourselves with the amazing spread the women prepared. Even Alex got a little mashed potato with cranberry sauce. Only a spoonful, though. When Vegas put his spoon away, Alex protested, until Vegas gave in and gave him another one. When it comes to presents, Alex probably got the most. Not that he was interested in them, he happily sat in the middle of the wrapping paper in his rocker, reaching out and playing with the paper. He's such a handsome little boy. He'll be trouble when he's older.

I look around the room, trying to locate Helen, but can't see her anywhere.

Until she walks in the door, followed by her bandmates, joined by Pennywise and Christmas. My eyebrows hit my hairline, and I'm not the only one dumbfounded in the room.

Raven walks over to them, chatting to Helen, before nodding and returning to Chloe, grinning his ass off. He whistles through his fingers, drawing attention.

"Brothers, Helen has organized a mini Christmas concert. Her band 'Silver' are joined by Christmas on drums and Pennywise on guitar."

Wow, I'm so proud of my woman. She's arranged all this on the down-low. I've heard of Silver before, and they are excellent.

After thirty minutes, they are all set up.

Helen takes the mike.

"Masher, this is my Christmas present to you. Raven, if you would come up here, please and hand out the words, so you can all join in?"

My heart pounds in my chest. *What is the minx up to now?*

Raven hands out the words to everyone but me.

Okay, she wants to serenade me? I'm totally fine with that.

The band jumps straight into "White Christmas", and I'm loving the rocky sound. Helen's voice rings as clear as a bell, and man, Christmas is awesome on the drums, flicking his sticks this way and that.

They follow up with "Fairytale of New York" as a duet by Helen and Pennywise, changing swiftly into "I Saw Mommy Kissing Santa Claus". We're all singing and clapping, enjoying the sounds.

I recognize the opening cords of "Jingle Bells" but howl with laughter when Helen sings,

"Jingle Bells
Alex smells
Ashley ran away

Oh, what fun it is to change
Alex every day, oh
Jingle bells
Alex smells
Vegas holds his nose
Hosing Alex
Cleans him best
Now he's smelling like a rose."

By this time, I'm crying with laughter, and the applause is thunderous. I can't hear myself think with all the whistling, clapping, and feet stomping. When did she find the time to do something like that?

"I've got another one." She smirks right at me.

Uh oh, suddenly I feel like a deer in the headlights.

The music starts and Helen's sultry voice breathes:

"Masher the red nosed biker,
Had a very shiny nose, and if you ever saw him,
You would know its moonshine glow

All of the other bikers,
Used to rib him anyway
They never let poor Masher
Forget about his moonshine ways.

Then one snowy Christmas Day

Raven came to say,

Masher with your nose so bright,

Won't you guide our ride tonight?"

"Oh, how the brothers ribbed him

Singing all with Christmas glee,

Masher, the red nosed biker

Your moonshine nose makes history."

Please ground, open up and swallow me.

The screeching, howling, and foot stomping have no end. My woman is an evil, wicked witch of a firecracker. But I love her anyway.

"I got another one for you." She smirks. "Don't think you'll all get away scot-free!"

"On the first day of Christmas, the bikers gave to me:

One Raven crowing, and a club under the Christmas tree"

"On the second day of Christmas, the bikers gave to me:

One Raven crowing, two bikers laughing and a club under the Christmas tree."

I rip the sheet Raven handed out earlier out of Zippy's hand, who is hanging over the side of his chair, collapsing with laughter, and look at the words.

3. two Prospects slaving
4. four Old Ladies cackling
5. five members drinking
6. Ally chasing Spark
7. one Vegas fainting
8. Slender beating Ratchet
9. Alex being naughty
10. ten bikes roaring
11. Masher in the chimney
12. A new pool table

And a club under the Christmas tree.

I'd like to say I'm pissed with her, but hell, this shit is funny.

"Last one for tonight, folks. I hope you enjoyed yourself as much as I have. Masher, I love you, but you've given me just too much ammunition," she cackles.

The music starts and I dread what I now know is coming.

Not just Helen and the band, but the whole club stands and joins in.

"When Masher got stuck up the chimney,
He began to shout
"Oh hell, I'm stuck

How can I get out?

Please, just help me out!"

"My beard is black

There's soot on my sack,

My dick is tickely too.

When Masher got stuck up the chimney, his balls were turning blue!"

I can't help but laugh until my belly aches and tears stream down my face. That woman, the Devil incarnate but sweet as pie. I'll love her until my dying breath.

When she finally walks towards me, I lift her and swing her around, draping her over my knee and kissing her soundly.

"You'll be the death of me, woman." I laugh when we come up for air to the shouting and ribbing of the club.

I throw her over my shoulder, her little hands smacking my back, but laughter pealing from her.

Walking towards the door, I call out, "Show's over, folks! Merry Christmas, everyone!"

The End

Printed in Great Britain
by Amazon

55310440R00076